THE SILVER CITY BRIDE

CYNTHIA WOOLF

FIREHOUSE PUBLISHING

Published by Firehouse Publishing
Woolf, Cynthia

Cover design copyright © 2020 Lori Jackson Design

CHAPTER ONE

*M*arch 20, 1863

*M*arch in Ft. Worth, Texas was supposed to be winter but tell that to the heatwave outside. At least with the sundown now, it would begin to cool off.

Eve Coleman sat at the poker table in her lucky red dress. The style was off the shoulder and showed enough cleavage to distract most players for a while. Not that she needed to distract them to win, she knew how to play poker better than most men, with five-card draw being her favored game. She'd play stud, if that was the only game in town, but she felt more comfortable with draw.

This saloon was a little run down, but it was full —standing room only. The chair she sat on was just wood, no upholstery but sturdy. She managed to get the chair with her back to the wall, as the scent of stale beer and cheap tobacco filled the air. Eve played at the table with four men. The man on her left was the only one that was clean and he was handsome to boot. The other three men were as filthy as could be. She was surprised a cloud of dust didn't follow them in when they sat down.

She'd pulled her long blonde hair into combs behind her ears, letting the curls fall down her back. Eve hated using the iron that made the curls, but the men seemed to like them better than her stick-straight hair. She used to color her lashes with coal dust and mineral oil to accent her eyes but stopped when she'd gotten a sty that made her take a break from poker while it healed. Now she used only the mineral oil on her eyelids to add shine and accent her green eyes. Eve had her mother's eyes but Helga Coleman never wore rouge on her cheeks or lips nor did she put anything on her eyes.

"You're beautiful without all that nonsense," her father had told her mother every time she suggested putting some on before they had gone out.

The corner of Eve's lips turned up just the slightest at the memory of her parents.

"What you smiling at, girlie?" asked the man across the table, teeth brown from chewing tobacco.

Eve smiled wider. "Just a memory. It's your bet. You in or out?"

"Don't be so bossy, girlie. I be thinkin'."

"Well, don't think too long." Under her breath, she whispered, "You'll get a skull cramp."

The dandy next to her chuckled. "That's a good one."

She turned and gave him a nod. He was a handsome man, with dark hair slicked straight back from his forehead, light blue eyes with dark lashes and eyebrows that slashed over them. He was clean shaven with a small cleft in his chin.

He reminded her of Johnny, her ne'er-do-well husband. He'd gone west for the gold, he said. He'd return a rich man, he said. He'd not actually done either. Moses Gunter shot him dead when he found Johnny in bed with Moses' wife who he also shot dead. Moses was hanged for those killings, defiant to the end.

The trap door had opened then and Moses dropped through, the rope breaking his neck. Three people dead and her a widow at eighteen, forcing her to find a job she could make a living at. Poker was it.

"Hey, Buck you remember that whore last night?" The man with the blonde hair grinned.

"Yeah, thought we'd pay her for a tumble." The

man with the Brown Teeth laughed. "Turns out she paid us. Ain't that right boys?"

"Right, Buck. She was a sweet little thing, too. Brandi was her name. I feel kinda bad takin' her money like we did."

This man was as unshaven as Brown Teeth was, but he seemed a little cleaner with a red bandana tied around his neck. Maybe that helped him sweat less. And at least his teeth were only yellow, not brown.

Brown Teeth laughed again. "She shouldn'ta kept it behind that dresser where we could find it."

Eve's eyebrow cocked up. "You robbed a poor prostitute?"

"She had it comin'," snarled Brown Teeth. "Wanted us to pay to ride her. I don't pay for no woman."

"That was her business, so you're expected to pay or you don't go in." Anger filled her but she masked it, just like she did all her emotions. Poker was no place for emotion. She leaned back and put an arm over the back of her chair. "But you know that, don't you? What did you do to her so she wouldn't tell her employer? Did you beat her up, too? Three such big strong men and one little whore."

"Shut yer trap, woman." He showed his bottom teeth in a snarl. "What you doin' here playin' a man's game anyway? They should bar women from here." Brown Teeth looked around the room.

THE SILVER CITY BRIDE

"The owner won't kick me out. I pay him good money to let me play. So, you can complain all you want." *As much as I tried to be who my father wanted, I appreciate him teaching me how to play. I can support myself this way and not have to prostitute myself.*

The handsome player also sat back and removed the gun he wore in a holster strapped to his thigh.

Eve removed the derringer from the pocket on her dress and aimed it at Brown Teeth. She'd had the dressmaker put a pocket in just for her gun. It was plenty long and wide so she could get her hand in and palm the weapon.

Handsome suddenly looked extremely dangerous with the weapon out. Despite her lack of emotion on the outside, her pulse raced and she was glad he was on her side.

"Maybe I'll teach you a lesson, myself." Brown Teeth stood.

Handsome pulled the gun up and pointed it at Brown Teeth.

Chairs scraped the floor as men at the other tables moved to get out of the way.

Eve didn't move.

Handsome's weapon never wavered. He narrowed his eyes. "If you want to live, either sit back down and play cards, or you and your friends take your leave. Now."

"We can take him, Buck."

This man had filthy blond hair that hung lank in front of his ears and on his shoulders. Blondie started to reach for his gun.

Handsome shot the man's hand and just as quickly pointed the pistol back at Brown Teeth.

Brown Teeth sat. "Guess we'll play some more." He looked at Eve through narrowed eyes. "We'll meet again, girlie and you won't have this dandy to protect you then."

The smell of gunpowder wafted past her nose. "Who said I need him to? But," she turned to Handsome. "Thank you for coming to my aid."

He smiled, his straight, white teeth almost sparkling in comparison to Brown Teeth. "Anytime, my dear. Anytime."

Eve decided then and there she would take all the money these three had. And the way these three played, she didn't have to cheat to do it.

She pulled her hand out of her pocket letting the derringer go. Then it was her deal. She shuffled and let Blondie cut the deck. Then she dealt the cards and they played.

After thirty minutes she'd stripped the men of the money they played with. She hoped they were playing with more than just poor Brandi's cash.

She raked the last pot in, put it in her reticule and then stood. "Well, gentlemen, time for me to call it a night. I hope to see you all in here tomorrow night as well." Eve looked down at Handsome, still in his chair, and winked.

He stood, took her left hand in his, and kissed the top. "Thank you m'dear. I haven't been so entertained in a long time."

She grinned. "You're more than welcome, kind sir. I appreciate your assistance earlier."

"Again, it was my pleasure."

"You cheated," shouted Brown Teeth as he slammed his hands on the table. "I want my money back. Now."

Eve turned to face the ugly man. "I didn't have to cheat to beat you or your friends. Now, if you'll excuse me." She turned away. As she did she heard the distinct click of a gun being cocked. She set her jaw and turned slowly.

Handsome had his gun leveled again.

Buck had his gun at waist height, aiming directly at Eve. Shots were fired and Eve fell to the floor, the wood planks scraping her elbows. Her heart lodged in her throat and her pulse raced. Getting shot at was definitely not a part of her regular day. From under the table she saw Brown Teeth's body land on the floor across from her.

"Don't shoot us, mister," said Red Bandana, his hands up away from his guns. "We don't agree with Buck. The lady won fair and square."

Blondie, also with his hands up, nodded so fast Eve thought his head would fall off.

Handsome leaned over her. "Miss, are you all right? Are you injured?"

Eve sat up, her reticule with her money in it, still in her hand. "No. I mean yes, I'm fine."

"Let me help you." He extended a hand and pulled her to her feet.

"I believe he would have shot me if not for you. Thank you, again. It seems I owe you a debt of gratitude. Normally, I don't have this much excitement when I play cards. I've been here for two weeks and never incurred such behavior."

"Nonsense, you owe me nothing. But if you insist, you can accompany me to supper. The food at the Carolina Rose, where I'm staying, is quite good."

"I'm staying there, too. And I agree about the food. All of my meals have been quite lovely." *I've been there for two weeks. Why haven't I run into him before now? Is it perhaps because our schedules are similar? Still it would have been nice to have someone to eat with before now.*

The owner ran up. "I saw what happened, Miss Eve. I'll have some men take him to the doctor."

"Thank you, Mr. Butler. As much as I think these men are scum, I hate the thought of being the cause of someone's death."

Handsome escorted her away from the table and

through the throng of men gathered to watch the hoped for carnage. He acted like this happened all the time and continued with their conversation. "I do hate eating alone, and I planned on walking you to your abode anyway." He tucked her hand in the crook of his elbow.

She liked his manners, being treated like a lady was nice for a change.

The poker table they were at was close to the bar and the walk to the door was a straight shot with tables on either side.

He patted her hand. "We'll simply kill two birds with one stone, getting you safely home and eating as well."

She looked behind them at the man on the floor. "What about Brown Teeth?

Handsome furrowed his brows together. "Brown Teeth?"

"Yes, the man you killed back there." *This isn't the first time I've seen someone die at the poker table. I refuse to get upset by it anymore.*

"Oh, I didn't kill him, provided his friends get him to the doctor. I shot him in his upper right chest. With a doctor's help, he'll survive."

"That doesn't bode so well for us. He thinks I cheated him—"

The man grinned. "Which you did not. I watched you…carefully."

She chuckled. "I have to admit I thought about it, I feel sorry for that poor woman. Now, I just have to find her. How many Brandis could there be in whorehouses in Ft. Worth?"

He steered them toward the Carolina Rose, about three blocks down the street from the El Dorado Saloon where they'd been plying their trade. "Probably more than you expect, but I happen to be friends with most of the madam's in this town and only one Brandi could be described as a little thing, as that filthy man said."

Eve looked up at him, an eyebrow raised. "Why am I not surprised you would know where to find her? This is her money, not mine."

"After you tell me your name. I don't want to keep thinking of you as The Blonde."

Eve laughed. "I've been calling you Handsome in my mind."

"Thank you for thinking me handsome. Daniel Calhoun, at your service."

Outside the saloon, the air was cooler due to the breeze and there weren't all the people crammed together.

"Eve Coleman." Eve appreciated the fact they didn't have to yell at each other to be heard, even as they passed other saloons, tinny piano music coming out their open doors.

"Beautiful name, Eve."

She nodded and tried her best not to lean into the man. It was a long time since she'd talked to a man other than to play cards. "It's my grandmother's name. My father's mother. She's long gone now."

Daniel patted her hand. "I'm sorry for your loss."

Eve chortled. "Don't be. She was a nasty old witch, who delighted in scaring me nearly to death. And I her only grandchild."

He grinned. "Well, I guess I'm not sorry for your loss."

"Thank you, just the same."

They arrived at the Carolina Rose and walked through the lobby to the restaurant. A young, brunette woman with spectacles held a menu and stood at the entrance to the dining room.

"Two for supper, Mr. Calhoun?"

"Yes, Bea, and a table in the back of the room, if you please."

Daniel slipped the woman a sum of money.

She brightened right up.

"Yes, sir. Right this way."

Eve chuckled. "You must have a way with women. They don't like to let me in here, dressed as I am."

He looked her up and down, then grinned. "What's wrong with the way you're dressed?"

She tilted her head and cocked a brow. "You're teasing, right?"

He laughed. "Yes. I happen to like your dress, but the *ladies* of this town probably are jealous."

Bea showed them to the table.

Daniel held out Eve's chair and turned to the waitress. "Thank you."

"Of course, sir." She left the menu on the table.

Eve picked it up. "Not many choices, but then they don't need many."

"I agree."

She handed him the menu. "I'll have the trout."

"Good choice. I'm having the steak. Now that we have that out of the way, I should tell you that gang will come gunning for you regardless if Brown Teeth dies or not. Apparently, they are brothers."

Eve took a deep breath and then released it slowly, her stomach roiled at the thought of being chased by Brown Teeth and his brothers. "I was afraid of that."

"I have a suggestion if you don't mind me commenting."

"Not at all. I know I'll have to leave town, but I'd like to have some protection, too."

"Then I suggest you become a mail-order bride and lay low for a while."

She laughed quietly. "Me? A mail-order bride? I wouldn't have any idea where to start."

"Start with the advertisement in today's paper. A

judge in Silver City, in the Nevada Territory, is looking for one. It will take about a month

to get there, but it's probably your best chance of losing them."

"Thanks, I'll get the paper. Tell me, why did you help me beat them? I saw you fold on a couple of winning hands and let me win. Second, why on earth would you be reading the ad in a newspaper about mail-order brides?"

"I always end up reading the entire paper cover to cover between games for something to do. As to helping you, I didn't like hearing what they did to Brandi, either. I'm glad you got her money back. I'll find out where she works and I have a copy of the paper in my room, if you'd like it."

"Thank you. You're being awfully nice to me. Why?" *I know why, but I want him to admit it. He's not the first man to buy me supper with the expectation that I will let him bed me and just because I'm a gambler and spend my time in saloons.*

He placed his hand over hers on the table. "It's not a secret. I'd like to bed you."

She pulled back her hand, not wanting to give him any encouragement. Eve pushed her chair back. "I'm sorry Daniel. I'm a gambler, but only with cards, not with my body."

Daniel nodded. "As you wish." Then his smile

returned. "Please, I'd still like for you to have supper with me. I really *don't* like eating alone."

She scooted her chair back toward the table and then rested her forearms on the table edge and clasped her hands together. "Neither do I. Sleeping alone is another matter."

He reached for her again. "I understand."

She let him take her hand, even moved her hand forward so she had her elbow on the table. "Will you still help me find Brandi?"

He furrowed his brow. "Of course. My finding Brandi was never determined by whether or not you let me make love to you." He squeezed her hand and released her.

"I appreciate that." Eve moved her hands to her lap, grabbing her napkin and placing it in her lap.

Their waitress returned.

"What will you folks have tonight?"

They gave her their orders and asked for coffee to be brought immediately.

She returned with their coffee and a small pitcher of cream.

Eve put cream and sugar in her coffee, not knowing what to say now and yet the silence was not uncomfortable.

"So, Eve," Daniel began once their meals had arrived. "How did you become a gambler?"

"When my parents were killed, I had to find a way

to make a living. I was a widow and an orphan by the time I was twenty. I didn't know how to do anything really. I'm a terrible cook, or so my husband said, and though I can do housework, I hate it. My daddy played poker to support us and taught me to play, too." She waved an arm taking in the town. "So here I am. Playing poker for a living and it's a nice living. I'm good at it, but I noticed so are you. So you play professionally, too?"

Daniel took a bite of steak, chewed, and swallowed before responding. "I do so I recognized a kindred spirit in you when I saw you playing so well. Watching you work was like watching a surgeon making precise movements to remove a limb. You took a few pots from me and that's unusual, unless I want it to happen, so the chumps will fall into my trap. Sort of a spider and fly scenario."

Eve enjoyed her meal. The chef had deboned the trout and removed the backbone so the fish lay flat, then he'd broiled it with lemon butter. It was delightful.

When she was done, she placed her utensils crossed on the plate and pushed it away. She'd eaten everything as she always did. She often played such long games that meals were forgotten.

"You have quite the appetite, dear Eve. I like a woman with a good appetite for all things."

Eve laughed. "You are a charmer, Daniel Calhoun."

They both finished their meals and Daniel pulled back Eve's chair. He left money on the table for the waitress.

Eve walked with Daniel to his room for the paper. She waited in the hall.

He handed her the newspaper. "Are you sure you won't change your mind about staying tonight?"

She smiled. "I'm sure. Thank you for the offer. It's very flattering." Eve held up the paper. "Thank you."

Daniel leaned against the doorframe. "Anytime. I hope you enjoy Silver City."

Eve cocked her head and smiled. "I think I just might."

CHAPTER TWO

*B*ack in her room, Eve looked through the paper until she found the ad that Daniel had mentioned.

Wanted: One woman of exceptional character as mail-order bride for lonely man. Upstanding citizen, educated, some say handsome. Respond to Judge Earl Ralston, Silver City, Nevada Territory

She tore out the ad and put it in her reticule. *Well, he sounds interesting. A judge. Can I stand to be married to a judge? Can I give up gambling? My character is probably not exceptional in most people's estimation, but I'm a woman of good moral character. That will have to do.*

Before I leave I must find Brandi. In the meantime I'll send the judge a telegram to let him know I accept and will be there in approximately one month.

I wonder if he's old. Aren't all judges old? Can I handle being married to an old man?

The following morning Eve was eating breakfast when she saw Daniel enter the hotel restaurant and waved.

He smiled and walked to her table.

Today, she was in a plain, pink cotton dress that buttoned up to the neck and had her hair in a bun at her nape.

When Daniel reached the table, she pointed to the empty chair across from her. "Please join me."

"I'd love to." He sat and waved for the waitress.

The same young woman from last night appeared tableside. "What can I get for you folks today? The special is biscuits and sawmill gravy with two scrambled eggs."

"I'll take the special, with coffee and cream," said Eve.

"The same for me," said Daniel.

Bea wrote it on a pad. "Got it. Be right back with the coffee."

Eve turned her attention back to Daniel. "I tore out that advertisement. I hope you didn't want the paper back."

"No, I don't. Will you go?"

"After I find Brandi. Can you talk to your friends today?"

"Actually, I visited her last night. She's quite a mess from the beating she received. I also learned, through some scuttlebutt in one of the saloons, the men are the Stone brothers, Buck is the one I shot and the oldest, followed by Jack and Billy is the blond and the youngest. According to my source, they are some bad men, wanted for many crimes in several states, including murder. The sooner you leave town the better. I'm planning on doing that myself as I'm sure Buck Stone will take exception to my shooting him."

"Oh, that's wonderful."

Daniel chuckled. "Yes, I thought I remembered a Brandi at my friend's establishment and she does. So, I asked if she was working and if I could speak to her."

Eve leaned forward. "Were you able to talk to her?"

"Yes. She's just a little thing and young, probably around eighteen or nineteen. She'd obviously been beaten, and she admitted the men who did it stole her money, too."

The waitress returned with the coffee and set a cup in front of each of them. "Where can I find her?" Eve poured cream in her coffee and added a sugar cube from the bowl on the table.

"She's at the Frontier Rose Brothel. I can take you

there after breakfast if you like. I told the madam I might be back today with a friend to talk to Brandi."

"That would be wonderful." *I've never been to a brothel. I am quite curious as to what one is like on the inside.*

They ate quickly and headed out to the brothel. It was about six blocks West from their location.

The walk took them past saloons and brothels with a few restaurants sprinkled in.

Eve was comfortable in a town like this one. Most of the towns she worked in were just like this, maybe smaller, but not much different. Now the saloons were quiet, the pianos silent.

When they arrived, Daniel rang the bell.

A brunette woman in scanty clothes answered the door.

He put a hand in his pants pocket. "We'd like to see Rose, please. We are expected."

"Sure. Come on in. I'll get her. Wait here." The woman headed down a hallway off the room where several girls lounged.

Eve and Daniel waited in what looked like a living room, with a couple of couches and comfy looking overstuffed chairs. She'd always wondered what a brothel was like inside. She hadn't known what to expect but this wasn't it. The girls looked like they were on display until a man picked them and took them upstairs.

A few minutes later a very buxom blonde, with obviously dyed hair, walked down the hall. She too was dressed in a negligee.

"Daniel." She sashayed up to him, her hands outstretched, palms down.

"Rose." He kissed the tops of both of her hands and then removed his hat. "This is the friend I told you about last night. Rose Smith, meet Eve Coleman."

Eve extended her hand. "Pleased to make your acquaintance."

Rose took it with both of hers and shook. "I understand you want to see Brandi. I'm afraid she won't be working for a while. Some drunken men beat her, leaving her covered in bruises."

Eve nodded. "Yes, that's what I want to talk to her about."

Rose looked over Eve's shoulder to one of the women lounging on the sofa. "Maude, go get Brandi, please."

Eve watched Maude return with a small, woman with light red hair who limped a little. As Brandi got close Eve saw her black eyes and cut lip. Those men had hurt her badly and she wished she could do more than just win back Brandi's money.

"You wanted to see me, Rose?"

"Yes, dear. These people would like to talk to you. Why don't you take them to the kitchen and give them some coffee?" Rose put her arm around Brandi's shoulders. "Go on, hun. Have some yourself and see if you can eat something. Breakfast is still in the warming oven."

Brandi shook her head and then winced. "Hurts too much." She turned her gaze to Eve and Daniel. "Follow me."

Brandi was several inches shorter than Eve and, if she didn't have the bosom she did, would look to be about twelve. *I wonder if that fact was more attractive to the customers?*

In the kitchen, Brandi pointed at the table. "Take a seat. I'll get the coffee." She returned with three cups of black coffee and gingerly sat across from Eve.

Eve didn't have the heart to ask for cream so she drank the coffee black. "Brandi, I'm Eve Coleman. Daniel and I are gamblers and ran into the men who beat you last night. They were bragging about stealing your money and thrashing you."

"So," she shrugged. "Doesn't matter now. It's gone, four-hundred-sixty-two dollars and fifty cents. I need five hundred to buy my contract from Rose and I can't work like this." She waved her hand in front of her face and torso.

Eve set her reticule on the table and then dug into it bringing out the bills. She counted out four-hundred-seventy dollars. "I won this from them last night."

"Actually," interjected Daniel into the conversation. "She took it from them. Eve here is quite adept at poker and it didn't take her long to outplay those animals to get your money back."

Eve clasped her hands on the table. "I have a proposition for you. I'll pay the rest of the money to buy your contract if you will travel with me to the Nevada Territory and I'll buy you new clothes for the journey. I don't like the thought of going alone. How old are you by the way?"

Brandi's eyes got wide and tears filled them. "I'm almost twenty-one. You would do that for me? Why?"

Eve's shoulders sagged a bit. She missed her parents and seeing Brandi had made her more thankful to her father than ever. Even though he hadn't known it then, he saved Eve from a horrible fate. "Because I could be you. If my father hadn't taught me to play poker, I would have had to become a prostitute to eat. So, what do you say? Shall we talk to Rose?"

Wiping her cheeks with her palms, Brandi nodded. "Yes, please. I'd love to travel with you."

Eve smiled and looked at Daniel. "Would you get Rose for me?"

"Delighted to." He stood and headed to the living room.

She turned to Brandi. "I'll teach you to play poker

so you'll never have to prostitute yourself again. Would you like that?"

"Oh, yes, ma'am. I would rather die than do this again, and I got lucky. Rose is a good woman."

"I'm glad to hear it," boomed Rose as she entered the kitchen followed by Daniel. She sat at the head of the table. "What can I do for you all?"

Daniel sat on Rose's left across from Eve.

Eve gathered the money on the table and counted out twenty-five dollars more. "I want to buy Brandi's contract."

Rose glanced at the money. She jutted her chin toward Brandi. "Done. Go pack your things and put some clothes on."

Brandi grinned wide and then grimaced, a hand flying to her lip. "Yes, ma'am." She hopped up from her chair and limped out of the room.

Rose narrowed her eyes at Eve. "What will you do with her? Start your own house?"

Eve shook her head and lifted her chin a notch. "No, actually, she'll be my traveling companion. After we reach our destination, she'll be free to do as she pleases."

The woman looked over at Daniel, then clapped him on the shoulder. "You know how to pick'em. She's a good one, Danny Boy."

Daniel blushed.

Eve assumed it was at the use of a private, and

amusing, nickname. Daniel Calhoun hadn't been a boy for a long time, which made Eve wonder how long he'd known Rose. It didn't matter. It was none of her business.

Brandi returned in about five minutes with a single carpetbag.

Eve couldn't imagine packing and dressing in that amount of time.

She was wearing a simple black skirt and pink blouse with high neck.

"Where'd you get those clothes, and where's the rest of your things?" asked Rose.

"I'm only taking the clothes that I've never worn. I was waiting for the time I could leave before I wore them. I got one more skirt, blouse, chemise, and bloomers. That's it. I couldn't afford no more and still save to buy my contract."

Rose threw her head back and laughed. "You're a smart one, Brandi Johnson. I'm proud to see you go. I think you'll go far."

Eve stood and extended a hand to Rose. "It was a pleasure doing business with you, Mrs. Smith."

The madam shook it. "It's just Rose. Mr. Smith is long gone."

Eve tilted her head and lowered her chin. "I'm so sorry for your loss. Please accept my condolences."

Rose waved dismissively. "Don't be. He ain't dead, at least, I don't think he is. He's just gone. I kicked him out for being a lazy, no-good drunk. I loved him, but he was bad for business. Caught him *testing* the girls. Can't have that now, can I?"

Eve raised her brows and widened her eyes. "No, I don't suppose you could. Have a good life, Rose."

Daniel stood, kissed Rose's hand, and put on his hat. "I'll see you again before I leave Ft. Worth."

Rose blushed like a schoolgirl. "I'm looking forward to it."

Brandi led the way out of the brothel, past the open mouths of the other prostitutes.

Maude stopped her. "I'm happy for ya, Brandi. Think kindly of me in your new life."

Brandi put down her bag and hugged the woman. "Don't worry about me, Maudie. I'll be just fine, and you will, too. Just keep savin' like I did. It took me moren' six years but I did it. I knew I would as soon as Miz Rose gave me a contract and you can, too." She hugged the woman again and then picked up her bag before turning to Eve. "I'm ready now."

They walked out into the street.

Brandi had a smile on her face despite her cut lip, her back was straight and her head held high.

Once outside, Daniel's gaze landed on Brandi. "Here, let me carry that. It may not have much inside but carpetbags are heavy in and of themselves." He took her bag.

Eve linked an arm through one of Brandi's.

"You'll stay with me tonight and we'll leave on the stage tomorrow. Today, we're getting you more clothes to put in that carpetbag. And we'll get the stage tickets to Silver City. I wired the judge who wants a mail-order bride, but I've never been there and don't know what to expect. Whatever it is, we'll be all right. I won't let anything happen to us."

More people were out and about now. It was midmorning and the late risers were out getting breakfast. Their steps clicked on wooden boardwalk beneath their feet.

Daniel walked next to the street with Brandi in the middle. "I think it would be prudent to get your tickets first. They might cost more than you are antic-ipating. You'll have to go northwest to Denver first which will take a minimum of eleven days, and then west to Silver City which will take at least another fourteen days. It's going to be an exceedingly long trip. As a matter of fact, I'd only buy the tickets to Denver here. Once you get there, you'll want a couple of days in town to sleep in a bed, have a bath or two and at least a couple of good meals before getting on a stagecoach again. Believe me, I know from what I speak, having made the trip to California and back more than once."

Eve looked over Brandi's head, since she was so short, to talk to Daniel. "That's a great idea. I wasn't looking forward to twenty-five days in a stagecoach.

But if we break it up, the trip won't seem so bad. If he's already married by the time we get there, I'll be back to gambling. I won't have any choice." She looked down to Brandi. "What do you think Brandi?"

"After the life I've lived for the last six years, ridin' in a stagecoach is nothin'."

Eve's heart went out to the girl. "You've had a hard life, and I hope to change that."

"You've already changed my life, Miss Eve. You bought my contract out of there."

She shook her head. "You did that. I just gave a little help."

"It would've taken me another year, maybe two, before I got that much more money. You saved me and I'll never forget it. Anything you need, that I can give, I will."

Knowing that the girl didn't want charity, Eve thought about it for a moment. "Can you cook?"

"Yeah, I can. The girls all took turns fixin' the food because Rose didn't want to hire a cook. So, if we wanted decent meals, we learned to cook."

She patted Brandi's arm. "Good. Maybe you can teach me how. I'm sure my husband will want me to know how to prepare at least a few basic dishes, and I was never a particularly good cook."

The first stop they made was at the stagecoach station, where they got their tickets. Daniel had been correct the tickets were fairly costly one-hundred-twenty dollars per ticket. Eve didn't mind spending the money, she had enough to last her for some time, but not enough for her to retire from the game.

Daniel walked with them to the first of the stores Eve planned on taking Brandi to.

When they arrived, he looked at the clothing in the window and turned to the two women. "Here is where I leave you, ladies. I wish you both the best in the future." Then he looked directly at Eve. "Watch your back. Who knows if, though I'm sure it will be when, those men will turn up again?"

Her pulse began to race at the thought of those men finding her. But surely they wouldn't find her when she was headed so far away.

"I will and thank you for all your assistance."

"You're welcome, dear lady. Brandi, take care and learn everything Eve will teach you."

"I will Mr. Calhoun. Thank you."

He turned and walked on up the street, disappearing around the corner.

Eve gazed down at Brandi. "Now, we'll get you some more underthings, then a dress or two." She looked down at Brandi's feet. "And a pair of new shoes."

She probably shouldn't be doing this, but the girl needed clothes and she had plenty of money. When she reached Silver City, if anything was awry, she could still stake herself in a game. And she and

Brandi would have a roof over their heads. But she would have a husband to take care of her and refused to think it would not work. Eve was nothing if not resilient.

Now that she was getting used to the idea of being married again, she hoped the marriage worked. She wouldn't be in love with this man like she was with Johnny, but her love for him had died as though she'd had a bucket of cold water thrown on her. She would never be hurt again by the unfaithfulness of a man... any man, husband or not.

CHAPTER THREE

*M*arch 22, 1863

*E*ve and Brandi boarded the stage to Denver and quickly grabbed window seats. Eve had done enough traveling by stagecoach to know those were the best seats to be had and, with the heat wave continuing, the breeze would be welcome.

Deciding it best to make friends with her fellow travelers, she asked, "Who else here is going all the way to Denver?"

The man kitty-corner from her was the first to speak. "I am. I'm Reginald Dempsey. I sell liquor to every saloon from Denver to Dallas."

Mr. Dempsey held his sample case in his lap. It

was rather large and intruded into the space of the child next to him. Luckily, the little blonde girl didn't take up much room.

The woman across from the child nodded toward her daughter. "She's Angela and I'm Martha Baker. We're meeting my husband in Denver. He just bought a farm east of there, and Denver is the closest stage stop."

The man across from Mr. Dempsey introduced himself by pulling a paper-wrapped sucker from his pocket. "I'm Samuel Jackson, and I sell candy to every merchant I can between Denver and Ft. Worth." He looked at Martha Baker. "Do you mind if she has a sucker? It's cherry flavored."

Martha smiled at the man. "That would be perfectly all right and is much appreciated."

Mr. Jackson handed the candy to Angela.

She tore it open and shoved it in her mouth.

"Angie, what do you say to the nice man?"

She looked down into her lap and took the sucker from her mouth. "Thank you, mister."

"You're quite welcome, child." He looked at Eve. "And where do you hail from, my dear?"

"I'm Eve Coleman, originally from Missouri, but now I make my living playing poker." She pointed at Brandi. "She is Brandi Johnson, my traveling companion and cook."

Brandi lifted her hand and wiggled her fingers in greeting.

"My dear," said Mr. Jackson to Brandi. "You must have been in a terrible accident to have incurred such bruises."

Brandi froze for a moment and then said, "Yes, sir, I was. I tripped and fell down an entire flight of stairs. I'm lucky I didn't break my neck."

"Oh, you poor thing. I hope you're not in too much pain," said Mr. Dempsey. "Whiskey is often used for a pain killer. I do have some samples here which you are welcome to if you need them."

"Thank you, sir," said Brandi. "But they barely pain me, they are just more colorful now is all."

"Gambling! That's not a decent pursuit for a woman."

Martha Baker's eyes widened and her back stiffened. The woman would probably not talk to Eve or Brandi the whole trip. That was fine with Eve, who leveled narrowed eyes at Martha. "I'm a widow, Mrs. Baker. Would you prefer I worked as a prostitute or a saloon girl, perhaps? What would you do if your husband died?"

Mrs. Baker stared at her hands in her lap. "Well, no, I suppose not." Then she looked up. "Couldn't you have been a maid somewhere? It would be much more respectable."

Eve lifted a brow. "Perhaps, but not nearly as

lucrative. And I don't want to be beholden to anyone for my living."

"I suppose you're right. Still, it's not proper," insisted Mrs. Baker.

Shrugging, Eve said, "You can think what you like of me. I know who I am and what I'm not. My moral character is quite intact." She looked at Brandi. "Do you still want to learn to play?"

Brandi nodded. "Oh, yes, please."

"Very well, the highest winning hand is called a royal flush and consists of the ten, jack, queen, king and ace, all of one suit. The four suits are hearts, diamonds, clubs and spades." Eve pulled a deck of cards from her reticule. The small bag contained some of her money, cards, and a handkerchief, though she was beginning to think it was a magic bag. She hadn't expected to get in it all she needed to. Most of her money was sewn into her two carpetbags.

Now, with all the purchases they'd made, Brandi carried two, as well.

Eve took fifty dollars and gave it to Brandi.

The girl looked at the money in her hand and then at Eve. "What's this for?"

"No one should ever be completely broke if they can help it. Besides, you might need to stake yourself in a poker game sometime."

The trip to Denver was uneventful, except for the cold. The closer they came to Denver the colder the

THE SILVER CITY BRIDE

weather got. However, Eve couldn't let the little girl feel the cold and so kept the same seats. This way, Angela was warmed by Mr. Dempsey and Brandi. The trip took the eleven days as stated by Daniel.

Except for teaching Brandi to gamble and for the ever-present cold, Eve might have slept. There was nothing outside the coach but dry prairie, dead brown grass, few trees, and fewer rivers. No wonder journalists called it the Great American Desert. She saw buffalo herds in the distance, but they didn't come near the coach.

They arrived in Denver in the afternoon of Sunday, April 4th. Eve was so happy not to be in the bouncing coach anymore. She felt like she hadn't slept for the entire eleven days they'd been traveling. She led the way to the Town and Country hotel near the stagecoach stop. It was a decent hotel, with hot baths and good food.

The hotel was three stories, with brick on the first story and wood on the second and third stories. The second and third floors were painted a pale yellow, and the shutters matched the dark green ones on the first floor.

As she and Brandi entered, she heard the girl's intake of breath. The hotel might be near the stage stop but location was all they had in common. The floors of the hotel lobby were covered in rich Oriental carpets with a dark blue background and stars, paisleys or other decorations. The walls were painted a soft blue with no wallpaper.

Eve walked to the front desk.

The young man behind the counter pushed his glasses up his nose. "May I help you, miss?"

"Yes, please. I'd like a room with two beds, and I want two baths sent up as soon as possible."

He kept looking at Brandi. "Um, yes ma'am." He turned the register around for her. "Please sign the register."

She signed and turned it back around toward him.

He took a key from one of the cubbyholes behind the desk. "Here is your room key. Your room is down the hall on the right. Room 109. Baths before supper. Anything else?"

"Yes, what time does the restaurant close?"

"It's open until eight o'clock tonight."

"Perfect. Send those baths right away, please."

"Yes, ma'am."

Eve went over to Brandi, who was sitting on the sofa.

Together, they walked down the hall to the room. Eve opened the door and was momentarily speechless. She looked at Brandi. "I didn't expect this. The rooms were quite different the last time I was here. This is beautiful."

The room was almost as splendid as the lobby had been. It had two small beds, a table with two chairs, a single nightstand between the two beds, a wardrobe, and a chest of drawers. An Oriental carpet covered the floor and the window curtains were heavy green wool and matched the bedspread on each bed.

Brandi circled the room, touching everything. "I've never been any place as nice as this." She ran over to Eve and crushed the older woman to her. "Thank you. Thank you for coming into my life."

Eve wrapped her arms around the girl enjoying the feeling of being hugged again. "It was a lucky day for both of us. Look, there's a table. We can play poker and see how well you remember our lessons. It's awfully hard to learn in a moving coach."

"I know. My back hurts more than when I was a whore."

Eve narrowed her eyes. "Don't ever let me hear you refer to yourself as a whore."

Brandi pulled out of Eve's embrace. "But I was."

"You were a prostitute and were paid for your services. A whore is not. In my opinion, that makes a world of difference. Now, we'll stay here for two nights and then get on the stage for Silver City. Agreeable?"

The girl nodded vigorously. "Oh, yes. I'm anxious to start our new life."

Eve took off her shoes, then plopped onto one of the beds, lay back, put her hands behind her head and crossed her ankles. "I love these beds they are so comfortable, or at least they seem so after a long trip."

Brandi sat on the other bed. "My gosh, I never slept in a bed like this one." She clasped her hands and looked at the floor. "Do you think we can get a bath before we go eat? That sounds even better to me than food."

Eve grinned. "I ordered them at the front desk when I checked us in."

A few minutes later a knock sounded on the door.

Getting up, Eve crossed the floor and then answered it.

Two men entered, each carrying a long, metal tub, followed by two more men, each with two buckets of steaming water.

"We'll be right back with more," said one of the men carrying the buckets.

The four of them returned, two with buckets of cold water and the last two with hot.

After the men left, Eve locked the door, put a chair under the doorknob and stripped out of her clothes. She picked up one of the cold-water buckets and poured the contents into the tub, then tested the temperature with her fingers. It was still hot but perfect to soak away the aches and pains from the trip.

Brandi also prepared her tub. "Ahhh," she said as she gingerly got into the still steaming water.

"Are you sure you put in enough cold water?"

"Oh, yes." Brandi leaned back in the tub, a washcloth on the tub behind her to protect her from the cold metal. "This feels wonderful on my sore body."

"I'm glad most of the bruises are gone. Including your black eyes. Now I can see that you have beautiful emerald eyes to go with that strawberry hair."

"My hair was actually blonde when I was little. My mama said it got redder and redder the older I got."

"Well, it's beautiful now. Do you need help rinsing it?"

"Probably. I've never tried to rinse it by myself. One of the other girls, usually Maudie rinsed it for me."

"If you wait until I get finished, I'll dry off and then help you."

"Of course. I'd appreciate it."

When both were dressed, they were too tired to go out of the hotel, as Eve thought they might be, so they went to the hotel's restaurant for what turned out to be a fabulous supper. Of course, anything that wasn't beans and bread would have seemed wonderful. But, in this case, they each had a steak with mashed potatoes and brown gravy, carrots glazed with honey and supper rolls that were soft, and fresh.

Eve couldn't have asked for a better meal. She was extremely glad they'd stopped over. She and

Brandi needed the rest after the eleven days on the stage with little or no sleep.

It's nice not to be alone. Maybe I'm lonelier than I thought.

***

y the time the two nights had passed, Eve and Brandi were well rested, well fed, and ready to continue on their journey.

This time, a great buffalo herd stopped them, and they had to wait for several hours before being able to move again. This was always a dangerous time. The horses could become skittish, or the buffalo could run over the stagecoach. They were lucky in that neither situation happened.

Crossing the mountains provided yet another challenge. Snow fell at the top, and the road became slick. The coach slid, and everyone inside seemed to scream at once with fear and surprise.

"It's all right, Miss Johnson. These stage teams and drivers are the best around," said Mr. Clarendon, a young man wearing a tweed suit with patches on the elbows, along with a wool cape. He sat next to Brandi and placed his hand on top of hers, where it lay in her lap.

She gently pulled her hand from him, her breathing still rushed from screaming. "Thank you,

Mr. Clarendon. I'm sure you're right, and we'll arrive on the other side of the mountains safe and sound."

"I'm sure we will. I've made this trip several times now. I'm a teacher, but I go back to Missouri to collect books and supplies for the children. Most of them can't afford to go to school if they don't have this help."

Eve smiled to herself. Mr. Clarendon was smitten, but it didn't look like Brandi returned the sentiment. Of course, she was skittish about having a real relationship with a man given her background, but Eve was sure she'd get over that for the right one.

*A*pril 23, 1863
        Silver City, Nevada Territory

*T*hirty-two days after leaving Ft. Worth, Eve and Brandi arrived in Silver City. The stagecoach driver helped Eve down the steps to the ground.

Mr. Clarendon now known as George, assisted Brandi.

Eve looked around and saw the stage stop was in front of the Silver City Hotel. It was made of brick and wood. As she looked around she noticed a lot of the buildings were brick or rock on the bottom level and wood above.

On one side of the hotel were three saloons. The Red Lily, The Silver Slipper and Ned's Place. All three were made of painted clapboard. The Red Lily was painted red, the Silver Slipper was white and Ned's place was also white. Eve wondered if all the buildings in town followed that idea of painting the building to match the name.

Eve watched Brandi with George and wondered if she had told him about her past yet. If she did, did he realize he'd probably lose his job because of Brandi's background?

She sighed. Even though she was only about five years older than Brandi, she'd had a much different raising. Her father was disappointed she wasn't a boy. He'd wanted to pass down his knowledge about gambling in general and poker specifically. He eventually decided Eve was good enough and began to teach her. Now, she'd put her knowledge up against anyone, anytime, anywhere.

"Excuse me, miss? Are you Eve Coleman?"

The deep voice rumbled through her, giving her goosebumps. She turned and looked up…way up… into the prettiest blue-silver eyes she'd ever seen. "Yes, I'm Eve Coleman and this is my friend, traveling companion and cook, Brandi Johnson. And you are?" She'd already noticed the badge on his chest.

He started to extend his hand and then set his thumbs in his front pants pocket instead. "I'm Cameron Neal. I'm the marshal here."

She thought sure he was about to shake her hand and raised hers in response, then when he changed his mind, she used that hand to shield her eyes from the bright sun. "That's good to know. Do you think you could point me in the direction of Judge Earl Ralston?"

The marshal crossed his arms over his chest. "The judge isn't coming."

Eve folded her hands in front of her. The marshal's square jaw was clenched. He was a handsome man who Eve thought from the set of his jaw, was also quite stubborn. "That's not what I asked. Can you direct me to the judge's office or do I have to find it on my own?"

He took a deep breath and ran a hand behind his neck. "I'm mucking this up. The judge isn't coming because he's not the one he ordered the bride for. I am."

Eve's heart pounded in her chest. *Married to the marshal! What's the matter with me? I was willing to marry a judge why not a marshal?* "I'm sorry to hear that."

He frowned and narrowed his eyes, the crow's feet becoming more pronounced. "Why? What's wrong with me?"

43

She lowered her hand and waved it as though shooing a fly away. "Oh, it's not you, it's what you do. I'm a gambler, Marshal Neal. I don't think a marriage between us would work."

His nostrils flared. "I see. You were willing to marry a judge, but not a marshal. I don't understand your logic, Miss Coleman."

"It's Mrs. Coleman and I admit it does sound strange but I thought I could give up my profession if I was married to a judge."

"And you can't give it up to marry the marshal? Well, you'll have to, at least, for a little while. And we will be getting married. I'm not letting my friend down. Not in his condition."

Eve narrowed her eyes. "What condition?"

"He's dying, Mrs. Coleman. Doc Whitaker says he can't do anything for him."

Eve hardened her heart. "I'm sorry for your friend. Can't you just tell him we're married?"

He shook his head. "He's insisted on performing the ceremony."

Her shoulders sagged as she expelled a heavy breath. "Well, heck."

"I see you understand the problem."

Brandi stepped forward. "Why don't you get married and then when the judge passes, you can have it annulled?"

Eve smiled and stood straighter. "Sure, that would

THE SILVER CITY BRIDE

work. Perhaps a marriage in name only for as long as needed." *Let's hope it's not for too long a time. I'm terrible thinking such a thing. What's the matter with me?*

The marshal shrugged. "I don't know. I don't think anyone knows how long that could be."

"I really am sorry. Losing someone you care for is exceedingly difficult. I know. I lost my parents when I was twenty and my husband, too, though he deserved to die."

He lifted a brow. "I won't ask how as I'm not sure I want to know."

Eve rolled her eyes. "Don't worry, I didn't kill him, though I might have if someone else hadn't done it for me. He was cheating on me. Probably my fault, at least he would have said so, if he'd had the chance. I'm sorry, that's probably a lot more personal information than you ever wanted to know."

The marshal was quiet for a moment. "I can't imagine anyone cheating on you."

Eve's face heated to pinpoints in her cheeks. "Thank you. That's quite nice of you to say."

Brandi took a step toward the marshal and stood straight. "Nobody better ever cheat on her, or they'll answer to me." She tapped her chest.

Eve smiled at her friend who was a little bit of a woman and couldn't fight off a flea. Still, she appreciated the sentiment. A long time had passed since anyone stood up for Eve Coleman.

"I'll keep that in mind, little lady."

The marshal was not so boorish as to mention Brandi's stature... exactly. "Shall we go see the judge? Might as well get the ceremony done and over with." Eve picked up her bags off the boardwalk in front of the hotel. "Oh, and you should know, Brandi stays with me. She's my friend and as I said, my cook. If you want to eat, you'll let her stay."

Brandi also picked up her bags from the boardwalk.

"I accept those terms. You are both now a part of my family. Here ladies, let me take those."

He took two bags in each hand, turned and started walking.

The direction was toward what she thought was the middle of town.

Good grief, what am I getting myself into?

CHAPTER FOUR

They walked right through town to a patch of homes just to the east. Silver City was quite small compared to Ft. Worth, though it probably had as many saloons. Practically every business they passed was a saloon. The way they were built, slapped together was more like it, someone just opened a saloon wherever they got the land to do it. A patch of houses was surrounded by saloons, though she did see where the homes were being built farther out of town and luckily the saloons were not following.

They passed the marshal's office and jail. It was bordered by a saloon on one side and a tobacco shop on the other. Most of the businesses catered to men. She did see a mercantile and around the corner was a butcher.

Finally, the marshal stopped outside the white picket fence of a two-story white house with light blue shutters.

Eve thought for a judge, the house rather unpretentious.

Cameron led them through the gate and up a gravel path between flower gardens, or what would be flower gardens in the spring. She knew this because of the rose bushes sprinkled throughout.

He stepped up to a wide porch with a table and four chairs on one side and a swing and rocking chairs on the other. Pausing for a moment, he knocked on the door.

A petite, gray-haired woman with spectacles answered. "Cam, I'm glad you've come. He'll be so happy to see you."

Cam set the bags down and hugged the small woman. "How is he holding up, Blanche?"

Blanche wasn't very tall, about the same height at Brandi. The top of her head only came up to Cameron's chest. Even Eve was taller, though she wasn't considered tall by any means. Still, she came up to his shoulder.

Blanche sniffled. "As well as can be expected. Your being here will cheer him up." She looked over at Eve and Brandi. "And I assume one of these young ladies is Mrs. Coleman, who you'll be marrying today."

Cam nodded. "That's the plan. I know Earl was anxious for this wedding to happen as soon as possible." He stepped to the side. "This is Eve Coleman and her traveling companion, Brandi Johnson."

Eve stepped forward and extended a hand. "I'm pleased to meet you and I'm sorry your husband is so sick. Perhaps he'll turn around."

Brandi waved at Mrs. Ralston. "Nice to meet you."

Mrs. Ralston peered around Eve. "You, too, dear." She straightened. "Won't you all come in?"

"Certainly." Cam entered first and then held the door open for Eve and Brandi.

"Thank you," said Eve.

"Thank you," said Brandi.

"Put those bags down there by the door." Mrs. Ralston pointed to the right. "And follow me. Earl is in the kitchen. I'm afraid you'll be taking your vows seated at the table. After, would you please help him back to bed? It's just too hard for me because he's so much bigger than I am."

Cam wrapped an arm around Blanche's shoulders and hugged her close. "You don't have to ask. I'm happy to do whatever I can for him."

Blanche led them into the kitchen.

The room was not as large as Eve expected it would be in a house this size. Across from the door to the living room was the icebox, sink and all the counter space, which wasn't much. Two cupboards, which matched the table, were on either side of the sink with cupboards or drawers below the counter.

A window, which appeared to look out into the backyard, was over the sink. On one end of the counter was the icebox at the other end was the door to go outside.

On the wall directly to her right was the table made of oak. Between the table and the icebox was the stove. Across the room from the stove was the back door and on the same wall were pegs for hats, coats, and gun belts.

Searching for something to say, Eve decided truth won out. "You have a lovely home, Mrs. Ralston."

Blanche waved her away. "Please, my dear, I'm Blanche. Mrs. Ralston was my mother-in-law. And thank you. I try to make it cozy for us."

Judge Ralston sat at the head of the light wood table on the wall just left of the door. The table sat six. Everyone took a seat—Brandi and Eve on one side, Cam on the other and Blanche across from the judge.

In Eve's opinion, though he didn't look well and was quite pale, the judge didn't look like he was at death's door either. But then again, she didn't know the man.

"I'm glad I get to perform this service before I

THE SILVER CITY BRIDE

go," said the judge. "I've wanted to see Cam married for years."

Cam' s jaw clenched. "I never wanted to marry, Earl. You know that. I won't live the kind of life my parents did. Fighting all the time, yelling. Calling each other names. I don't want to marry and endure that for the rest of my life."

The judge reached over and patted Cam's hand. "Most marriages aren't like that. Look at Blanche and me. We've been married nearly forty years, raised up four children, and almost never said a cross word to each other. It's work, son, no doubt about it, but a good marriage is worth the work.

"I knew your daddy and mama from the time before they were married. They fought even then. It was just the way they got along. Some people are like that."

The marshal pulled his hand off the table. "Let's just get this ceremony over with before you collapse in the chair."

Eve narrowed her eyes at the judge. Was he wearing face powder? *The man is pretending! And the marshal is too close to the situation. He doesn't even suspect that people he loves would pull this act.* She glanced over at Blanche who stared back, the look on her face pleading for Eve not to give away the ruse.

Now, the question was, did Eve want to marry

Cam? The answer was, she did. She came here to hide from the Stone brothers. That circumstance hadn't changed. Just the man she thought she was marrying. She gave a very slight nod to Blanche.

The woman visibly relaxed.

Eve would talk to her before too long and find out just what this ruse was all about.

"Come now. Let's get started. Oh, wait. Cam, you haven't introduced us."

"Sorry, Earl Ralston." Cameron straightened. "Meet Eve Coleman and Brandi Johnson. Now, can we start?"

"Hold your horses. I need my notebook." He patted his pockets until he found the small pad and pencil. "I need your middle names, please."

Eve spoke for the first time. "No middle name. Just Eve Coleman."

"And Cam, I know yours is Lee."

"You *should* know it, considering you and Blanche are my godparents."

Eve wasn't really surprised at this bit of information. He obviously cared deeply for the judge to be marrying her just to please the man.

"Okay, now, you two must hold hands."

Eve reached across the table to meet Cam in the middle.

They clasped each other's hand.

"Good. Now, we are gathered here in front of these witnesses to join this man and this woman in matrimony." He looked at Cam. "Do you, Cameron Lee Neal take this woman, Eve Coleman, to be your lawful wedded wife, to have and to hold, for richer or poorer, in sickness and in health, and to keep yourself only unto her for as long as you both shall live?"

Cam looked at her. His icy blue eyes meeting her deep green ones. "I do."

The judge nodded and smiled.

"Do you Eve Coleman, take this man, Cameron Lee Neal, to be your lawful wedded husband, to have and to hold, in sickness and in health, for richer and for poorer, to honor and obey, and keep yourself only unto him, for as long as you both shall live?"

Eve took her time answering, instead staring at Cam, trying to read his thoughts. Looking back and forth between the judge and Blanche, she saw the worried looks on their faces. Finally, she said, "I do."

The judge and Cam both let out obviously relieved breaths. Blanche smiled wide.

Brandi was almost bouncing in her seat.

"Then, by the power vested in me by the city of Silver City and the Territory of Nevada, I pronounce you man and wife. You may kiss the bride."

Cam released her hand.

To her surprise, he stood and walked around the

table to where she sat, reached for her hand, and tugged her to a standing position. Then he took her face between his palms and gave her the sweetest kiss she'd had in a long time, maybe forever. When he pulled back, she followed him. Not wanting the kiss to end, she leaned toward him before opening her eyes.

Smiling, Cam swiped his finger down the tip of her nose. "That'll have to do until later."

Eve's face heated, embarrassed by her body's traitorous response, especially when he didn't seem to have the same response to her. She released a long breath.

Cam put a hand on the judge's shoulder. "Let's get you back to bed, Earl, before the doctor hangs us both."

"Not yet." He chuckled and then coughed. "Blanche made a pie this morning hoping today would be the day Eve would arrive. Me? I didn't care. I've had pie every day this week—just in case she was on the stage."

Eve looked at him and lifted a brow.

He coughed again.

Like I'll believe it a second time in case I didn't the first, Earl? He and Blanche had some explaining to do, and as soon as Cam and Earl, left she'd find out what the scam was from Blanche. She'd been around gamblers and charlatans all her life and she could spot when something wasn't right.

Blanche stood. "Oh, yes, we must all have pie and coffee." She poured them all a cup of coffee, placed a small bowl of sugar cubes on the table and then an equally small pitcher of cream. Then she cut them each a slice of pie.

Eve noticed the piece she cut for the judge was half that of the slices for the rest of them. She didn't worry about him though; plenty of pie left after they took their leave and he could eat as much as he wanted.

The pie was served.

Brandi took a bite and then closed her eyes and looked like she was in heaven. "This is the best pie. I wish I could bake."

"I can bake," said Eve. "I'll teach you."

Brandi took a bite and nodded.

Silence reigned as they indulged their tastebuds with Blanche's excellent apple pie, Eve's favorite if the truth be known. She let the sugar and cinnamon melt together with the apples and the flakiest crust she'd ever had. Eve loved to bake and her crust never turned out like this.

Cam stood and clapped a hand on the judge's shoulder. "Let's get you to bed, Earl before Blanche has my hide."

Earl nodded and coughed for effect.

Eve lifted an eyebrow and almost laughed out loud but covered her mouth with her fingers to hide her smile. As soon as Cam was out of earshot, she turned to Blanche. "Okay, what's the deal here? Earl's about as sick as I am."

The woman reddened. "Please don't tell Cam. We want what is best for him and ever since Marian left him at the altar, he hasn't been interested in courting. That was six years ago and he hasn't so much as gone on a picnic with a woman."

"He must have loved her very much," said Eve softly. She felt a pang of hurt that Johnny never felt that way about her.

"I don't think so. They courted for only a short time before he asked her to marry him. She was young, eighteen, and he was twenty-seven. I think he just decided it was time to be married. Yet, he never tried again. You know, once bitten, twice shy. That's Cam."

"So, you decided to get him a bride." She leaned close and spoke low. "Did you ever think about the bride's feelings? About thinking you're wanted, only to find you're married to a man who doesn't want you at all. Did you think about that?"

Blanche slumped in her chair. "We didn't. We were only concerned with Cam. I know that now. I'm sorry."

Eve eased off. She hated causing others discomfort, hated bringing anyone pain. "I understand. I won't say anything if I don't have to, but I won't lie either. If he confronts me, I'll tell him. Understood?"

Brandi put her hand on Eve's arm. "He won't be able to stop himself from falling in love with you."

"Thank you. I honestly hope you're right." *Having someone love me would be nice for a change.*

The older woman brightened a little. "Yes, I understand and agree, totally. Thank you for not giving us away. At this point Cam would never forgive us. It's our hope that you will learn to love each other as Earl and I do."

Eve barked out a laugh. "That's not likely to happen."

"What's not likely to happen?" Returning to the kitchen, Cam came and sat at the table.

"Oh, nothing. I just don't think I can ever bake a pie as good as the one Blanche made for us." Eve turned to Blanche. "Thank you for the pie. Apple is my favorite."

Blanche smiled. "Oh, you're welcome, my dear. I'll give you the recipe."

"I used to love to bake but haven't in years. Brandi will be doing all the cooking. I'm a lousy cook."

"And I'm a good one," the girl added.

Cam leaned back in his chair, one arm over the

back. "We'll I'm glad one of you can cook. Lord knows I'm tired of my own efforts in that regard."

Eve stood. "We should probably get going. Cam still must get us situated in our new home. I'd like to hang my clothes before I have no hope to get the wrinkles out of them."

"Of course, my dear. I totally understand." Blanche turned her attention to Cam. "Will you be here for Sunday supper?"

He pushed back his chair and stood. "I don't see why not, assuming the job doesn't need me. The ladies and I will be here around two o'clock Sunday afternoon."

Blanche clapped her hands. "Oh, I'm so glad. It will be so nice to have some female company. Right now, I do the dishes after supper while the men discuss the local goings on. I want to discuss things with another woman."

"We never meant to exclude you, Blanche." Cam ran a hand behind his neck. "But I guess we never did anything to include you, either."

She waved him off. "Don't worry about it. That's the way I was raised. Men went to the living room after supper, and women stayed in the kitchen."

Eve watched the older woman and did feel sorry for her. How long had she felt left out? "Well, you won't be alone anymore. Brandi and I would love to help you with the dishes and dish up some gossip."

"There you see?" He smiled at Eve and then at Blanche. "Our getting married is like you getting a goddaughter, too." Cam looked over at Brandi, his smile still in place. "Actually, you're getting two of them. Shall we go, ladies? You need to see your new home, and Eve and I have some talking to do."

CHAPTER FIVE

*C*ameron walked with Eve and Brandi followed.

Eve held out her arm and looked back at her friend. "Come up here."

Brandi grinned and ran up where she locked arms with Eve.

"Don't you ever act as less than my friend," said Eve. "Just because you'll be doing the cooking, doesn't make you a servant. You're part of this family. You just do the cooking, and I do the cleaning."

Cameron looked over at the two women who had just become his family and smiled. Eve seemed to be a little firecracker, and Brandi would probably be a handful, too.

Yet he wasn't upset, not like he should have been. And why had one look at Eve changed his mind? He'd gone there to meet her and send her on her way, but when he saw her, he suddenly wanted to marry her more than anything. Sure, she was beautiful, but she looked like a nice person, although his experience as a marshal proved one couldn't really tell much about a person when just meeting them. Lord knew his instincts about women were wrong. Look at his relationship with Marian. She'd left him for his best friend and then they'd moved back east to somewhere in Connecticut. He wished them the best, and good riddance to both.

Now he was married to a woman whose beauty made Marian look plain by comparison, and he knew Marian was anything but. Yet Eve's beauty was different. Where Marian's had been harsh and angular, Eve's was soft, rounded.

"Cameron." Eve snapped her fingers in front of his face. "Cameron, are you with us?"

"What? Oh." He shook his head to rid it of his musings. "Sorry, I was thinking about my ex-fiancée and how you two are so different."

She cocked her head and looked forward. "Sorry I'm not the woman you want."

She sounded a little hurt. "No, you mistake me. I'm glad you're nothing like her. You're more beautiful than she was for one thing. If Earl and Blanche had to get me a wife, I don't think I could have done better."

"So, where is your house? We've been walking now for a bit and," she breathed in deeply. "We seem to be running out of town." She stopped to breathe. "Sorry the altitude here has me short of breath. When we stopped in Denver, we were similarly afflicted, weren't we Brandi?"

"Yes, we were." Brandi sounded a little breathless, as though she'd been running for a spell.

"What?!" He looked around him and began to laugh. "Apparently, during my musings, I passed right by my house. It's not far but we need to turn around."

She tried not to smile. "I wondered since I didn't think the city would want you living out of town."

They turned around and walked about two blocks back down the rocky terrain of the hill, the way they'd come.

Finally, he stopped and opened the gate on the white picket fence surrounding a small, white clapboard house with brown shutters.

Gardens had sprung on both sides of the path and rose bushes ringed the front yard around the fence perimeter. Some flowers in the gardens, had sprung leaves above ground. The rose bushes were beginning to turn green but didn't have any blossoms yet.

A single, large blue spruce stood in the middle of the yard to her right.

"Your home looks lovely. I see you like to garden," observed Eve.

"Not really. These gardens and plants were here when I moved in. The city had been paying for the upkeep, but now it's up to me."

"Don't worry, Cameron. My papa was a farmer. We had all kinds of gardens from fruit and vegetables to flowers and rose bushes. I can take care of these," said Brandi.

He shook his head. "You're already doing the cooking, I couldn't ask you to take care of the yard, too."

Brandi shook her head. "You're not asking. I offered. Big difference."

Cameron smiled at the young woman. "If you'd like to, that'd be fine with me. I'd appreciate it very much." He waved his hand in an arc toward the house. "Shall we go inside, ladies?"

"I do believe we shall," said Eve, as she took Brandi's arm.

Did she need the support?

*Inside, Eve found the house just as lovely as the outside had been. Cameron was clearly proud of his home. The living room had a large, braided rug. A sofa, done in a green brocade, sat on the edge of the rug and faced the large fireplace. On either end of the sofa was a Queen Anne-style chair upholstered in the same brocade material. In front of the couch was a coffee table, and between the sofa and the chairs stood tall, slender tables. All the tables were made of a light colored wood and appeared well taken care of.

"Do you have someone come in and clean?" asked Eve.

He shrugged. "Sometimes. A lady I know comes in twice a month and oils the wood with lemon oil. She also takes the rug out and beats it. I guess now that you're here, you can do those things."

Eve stopped and put her hands on her hips. "I did say I would do the cleaning, but that was before I knew you had a housekeeper. But I stand by my words and will clean the house."

"I think I'll just go find the kitchen." Brandi backed out of the room, then turned and ran.

Eve didn't blame her. This was about to be an argument. "Don't expect me to do the laundry. I don't do laundry. I send mine out. Do you have someone who does that job here in Silver City?"

He dropped their bags and put his hands on his hips. "What do you plan on doing with your time if you're not working about the house?"

"I plan on working at my profession."

His eyebrows came nearly together, his eyes

narrowed, and his mouth formed a flat line. "You plan on going back to gambling?"

She brought a hand up and looked at her fingernails. "Yes, I haven't said I'd give up my profession."

"You're my wife and until that changes, you won't be gambling. You can find another use of your time. Have Brandi teach you how to cook, learn how to do laundry, whatever. You can do anything but gamble. Don't you know how to do anything else?"

Eve thought about it a moment. He was probably right. If the Stone brothers were tracking her, the first place they'd look were the saloons and gambling halls. As much as it pained her, she'd have to wait to gamble again.

"I don't do anything but gamble and no, I don't know how to do anything else. I said I could clean. Anyone can clean a house. But other than that…well, I do know how to bake. One of the few lessons my mother was able to get me to learn."

He put his hands on his hips. "No wife of mine will be a gambler. I'm the marshal for goodness sake. How would that look?"

Eve crossed her arms over her chest. "I don't suppose that would be too good for your image around town, would it? Well, we both have our reasons for wanting this marriage and for now, I need it as much as you do. So, I won't be gambling." She uncrossed her arms and poked a finger in his chest. "For now."

"Fine," he took his hands off his hips and pointed toward the way Brandi had run. "Would you like to see the rest of the house? We can start with the kitchen."

"Fine. Following you."

He led her down a hallway and into a large kitchen.

Brandi was looking through the cupboards. She looked up when they entered. "We've got a lot to do to stock your kitchen, marshal."

"You can call me Cam, Brandi. We're not standing on ceremony here. We are a family now after all."

She grinned. "Yeah, I guess we are."

Eve looked around the kitchen. She figured, if she were a cook, it would be a nice place to work. A four-burner stove with pale green porcelain doors on the oven, fire box, and warming shelf dominated the kitchen. He had a decent-sized two-door icebox and a pump at the sink. A table and six chairs stood against the same wall as the entry door from the living room. Directly across the room from the stove was a door she supposed went to the backyard.

"Do you like it, Brandi?" She wasn't sure what she'd do if Brandi didn't like the room. She couldn't very well ask Cameron to change it.

"I love it." Brandi turned in a circle next to the sink. "What's not to like?"

"It's smaller than the one you're used to."

She shrugged. "Fewer people to feed. At Rose's, there were usually about fifteen people for each of the meals. And it seemed when I cooked even more showed up." Brandi walked to Eve and took her hands. "This is a great place for me to work. You worry about me too much."

Eve gave Brandi's hands a light squeeze and released her. "All right. Cameron, would you show us the bedrooms now, please?"

"Certainly, follow me." He walked out of the kitchen and back to the living room, where he picked up their bags. From there he led them down a short hallway with three doors along it. "This is the coat closet," he said passing the first door on the right. "This room will be Brandi's." He opened the second door on the right and entered a good-sized bedroom.

A double bed with carved wooden head and foot-boards stood against the wall across from them. On the wall to her right was a bureau, and to her left were a tallboy dresser and a commode with one long drawer, one door for the chamber pot and two smaller drawers next to the chamber pot.

"Will this room suffice?" asked Cameron.

Brandi grinned from ear to ear. She walked to the

bed, sat and then popped up again. "It's wonderful. I've never had my own room that was this big."

"Great." He dropped off her bags and turned to Eve. "Our room is across the hall." He stepped up to the door and opened it.

She and Brandi followed him into the room.

It was huge. The bed's head and footboards were just like those in Brandi's room, but the bed was bigger and longer to accommodate his height. The furniture matched that of the room across the hall except the bureau had a mirror attached and an over-stuffed chair sat under the window with a table next to it.

"This is a nice room. Where are you going to sleep?" asked Eve with a straight face.

Cameron's eyebrows shot up. "I'm sleeping here. What do you expect?"

Eve burst out in laughter. "I'm just kidding you. I know we're expected to sleep together. I want to discuss our arrangements before we go to bed."

"Fine, let's do that now." He set her bags on the bed. "Brandi, if you could give us a few minutes. Perhaps you could make coffee and we'll meet you in the kitchen after we get a few things ironed out."

"If you don't mind, I'd like to unpack. So, I'll start the coffee and then be back in my room if you need me."

Cameron nodded. "That's fine. We'll find you."

Brandi shut the door behind her.

Eve sat on the bed. "Do you want to start first? This conversation is more important than unpacking right this minute."

Cameron stood next to the door with his knee raised and his boot flat on the wall. "I want to know if you really want to annul this marriage after Earl dies."

"Why?" Rather than look at him she ran a hand over the patchwork quilt that graced the bed. The material was soft between her fingers as though it had seen lots of use before being made into the quilt. She finally turned her gaze on him. "Don't you?"

He shrugged. "I don't know. Before we married, I didn't think I'd ever want to get married, but now that we are, I find I like the idea of a wife and children. Do you want children, Eve?" he asked softly.

Do I want kids? "I honestly haven't given it much thought. I guess I wanted a family when I was married to Johnny, but we were never so blessed." She stood. "What if I can't have children, Cameron? What then? I make a good living at gambling."

"If that's the case," he pushed away from the wall. "Why become a mail-order bride? Why get married at all?"

"I'll be honest with you because you deserve that. When I was in Fort Worth, Texas, I ran across some bad men. They had used a prostitute, beat her up and then robbed her. They had the poor idea to boast about it while playing cards with me, so I played until I had all their money. They were stupid players so it didn't take too long to win all the money they had. They were none too happy about that and said I cheated. I didn't. I'm just exceptionally good at what I do. Another gambler at the table helped me. He, too, was appalled by their story and their behavior. Anyway, one of the men tried to kill me as I left the table and the other gambler had to shoot him." Her stomach soured at she remembered. "He didn't kill him, just made it so I had a couple of weeks head start before they came after me. I found the prostitute with the other gambler's help and returned her money. I even gave her the rest of the money to buy her contract."

His eyes widened. "Brandi? You're talking about Brandi."

Eve paced from the nightstand to the dresser and back again. "I asked her to come with me as my companion and to cook for me when I arrived. I didn't know for sure if I'd actually marry anyone. Anyway, Brandi is free now. She can do what she wants with her life. She can stay with me or go on her own or marry or anything she wants to do. I taught her how to gamble, so she won't ever have to become a prostitute again."

He pushed away from the wall and caught her as she passed. "You're a good woman, Eve."

"I try to be." She stepped away from him and sat on the bed again. "Anyway, the Stone brothers are probably after me and I thought being a mail-order bride might get them off my scent. So, there you have it. Why did Earl and Blanche want so badly for you to get married?" *Does he have the same explanation as to why they wanted so badly for him to marry?*

"Because, since Marian left me, I haven't ever taken an interest in another woman…until now."

She lowered her gaze so she looked at him through her lashes. "Why now?"

"Probably because you're already my wife. And I decided, when Earl was performing the ceremony, that I'd like to have that family and children I always thought I'd have."

She crossed her legs and placed her hands slightly behind her on the bed. "Even if we do stay married, I want to get to know you a bit before we consummate our vows."

"I suppose that's reasonable. Well, shall we go have some coffee and you can tell me what the Stone brothers look like? I need for my deputies to be on the lookout for them."

"All right, let's go."

I hope I'm making the right decision. What if we

can't stand each other, or worse, what if after a few days I learn what making love should be and he doesn't want me then? He's awfully handsome but that doesn't mean we'll get along. I don't even know if he has a good sense of humor. Lord, what should I do?

CHAPTER SIX

*T*hey found Brandi sitting at the kitchen table with a cup of coffee.

Eve guessed she and Cameron had been talking for longer than she thought.

Brandi looked up as they came in. "I was beginning to think I wouldn't see you two for the rest of the evening. I don't know about you, but I'm starving. Eve and I haven't eaten anything since last night except the pie at the judge's house."

"Well, I guess I ought to feed you ladies. You'll have to go shopping tomorrow." He got two cups and the coffee pot and brought them to the table.

"Definitely. You have almost nothing to cook in this house. Eggs and bread. Which we can have if necessary."

"Brandi and I both need baths tonight as well," said Eve as she sat across from Brandi.

"Oh, yes, I can barely stand myself," said Brandi.

Cameron sat at the head of the table. "We'll, why don't we go get something to eat and then you ladies can have a bath? Although, the quickest way for you both to get a bath would be at the bath house. That's what we should do and then we can go to supper after. What do you say?"

Eve looked at Brandi. "I haven't been to a bath house in ages but I think it's a great idea. I don't relish going into a restaurant like this." She waved her hand up and down her front.

Brandi nodded. "I agree. I'm not used to going without a bath every day. I laid out my clothes on the bed so they should have had some time to become a little less wrinkled."

"Mine are still in my bag, but I don't care. Wrinkled or not, at least they're clean."

Cameron stood. "Okay then let's head to the bath house. I suggest you use one carpetbag for both of you and get a room with two tubs."

"You know an awful lot about the bath house," said Eve.

"I'm the marshal. I must know about the businesses in town. Besides, when I first moved here, I used it a time or two myself."

"Well, that makes sense. Let me grab my dress

and undergarments. Brandi, we'll put them in one of your bags since they're empty right now. Be right back."

Alone in the bedroom, Eve took out her pink calico dress. It wasn't too plain or too dressy. She thought the marshal would appreciate her thoughtfulness.

A timid knock sounded on the door.

"May I come in?" Brandi stood in the doorway.

"Of course."

"Here's my bag...ready for your clothes." Brandi set the bag on the bed.

Eve put in her dress, bloomers, and camisole. Her skin had too many sores from the corset she was wearing to put another one on after she bathed. "Okay, let's go. I can't wait for that bath."

"I know, me too. I haven't gone that long without a bath in years. When you're a whor...I mean a prostitute, you bathe a lot."

Eve closed the bag and walked to the living room, followed by Brandi.

Cameron waited by the door. "You ladies ready?"

"More than ready," said Eve.

"Yes, sir. I can't wait."

Cameron took them to the bath house and introduced them to the proprietor. "Jed Smith, this is my wife, Eve, and our friend, Brandi."

"Pleased to meet you, ladies."

"You, too," said Eve as she took in Jed's appearance. It was her habit to take in a person's appearance and name so she would know them if they sat at the table with her. *Average height, black hair, parted in the middle, well-groomed beard and mustache.* "Can we get a room with two tubs, please?"

"Surely can." He took a key off the wall and handed it to Eve. "Room three down the hall."

"Thank you." She turned to Cameron. "See you in about thirty minutes or so."

When they emerged from the bathhouse, Cameron was waiting.

"Well, ladies, how do you feel?" asked Cameron.

"Fantastic," declared Eve.

"Terrific," said Brandi.

"Great. It's early enough, the mercantile won't be closed if we have a late lunch first and then go there, if you'd like to get food tonight."

"Sounds good," said Brandi. "I'd like to get food for supper tonight at least. We can go back for regular shopping tomorrow."

"Fine by me," said Eve. "I'm starving."

"Me, too," said Cameron.

He picked up the bag with their dirty clothes.

"You ladies clean up real nice." He turned away and started walking up the street back toward his… no, their…home.

Cameron took them to The Nugget Café for a late

lunch. "It may not look like much, but the food is good."

"That's all that matters to me," said Eve. "I've eaten in plenty of dives that had great food and fancy restaurants with just mediocre fare."

"I'd never eaten in a restaurant," admitted Brandi. "Until we were in Denver on the way here. It was very good. I'll be glad of the food here no matter what it tastes like."

"You'll be pleasantly surprised," said Cameron. "I guarantee it."

The Nugget was a typical café. Red checked tablecloths graced the square tables. A sugar cube holder sat in the middle of each table along with silverware for four people.

The dark haired waitress showed them to a table in the back. Cameron held Brandi's and then Eve's chair before sitting with his back against the wall.

"I usually sit with my back against the wall," said Eve. "I imagine for the same reason that you do."

"I don't want anyone to get the drop on me," replied Cameron.

Eve nodded. "Exactly."

The waitress came back with menus and passed them out. "Do you want something to drink?"

"I'd like coffee with cream," said Eve.

"Coffee, black," said Brandi.

"My usual, Janie."

"Sure thing, Cam. Coming right up, ladies."

"I'm surprised to see a young woman here. I thought there weren't any women and that's why you needed a mail-order bride."

"Not many single women. Janie and her husband own The Nugget. Most every woman you'll meet is married and usually not to a miner."

The woman returned carrying a tray with cups and saucers, a cream pitcher and the coffee pot.

"Janie. This is my wife, Eve, and our friend, Brandi." Cam waved his hand between Eve and Brandi.

"Pleased to meet you both," said Janie.

"I'm happy to make your acquaintance," said Eve.

"Hi," said Brandi.

Janie took a pencil and pad out of the pocket of her once white apron. "Do you know what you want to eat? The special today is an open-faced roast beef sandwich with mashed potatoes and gravy, green beans and peach cobbler for dessert."

"I'll take that." Eve set her menu on the table.

"Me, too," said Brandi.

"Make it three," said Cameron.

"Well, you all make my life easy." Janie picked up all the menus. "Be back shortly with your meals."

She returned in no time, carrying the three plates and the coffee pot. Janie set the coffee pot on the floor then placed a plate in front of each of them. "More coffee, folks?"

Everyone said yes.

She refilled the cups.

When they finished eating, she was right there to pick up their plates and then bring them the dessert.

The peach cobbler was the only thing Eve was disappointed in and then only because she knew she could bake one that tasted better.

"It's still early," said Brandi. "This meal won't last us until tomorrow morning."

"I'll take you to the mercantile, baker and butcher. You can get food for supper and then tomorrow you can come back for a more extensive shopping trip.

After they left the cafe, he carried their bag and took them first to The Silver City Mercantile. A bell sounded when they entered.

"Hi, Carl," called Cameron. "I want you to meet my wife, Eve, and our friend and cook, Brandi Johnson."

Carl came around from the behind the counter and held out his hand. "I'm pleased to meet you, Eve."

They shook hands. Carl was average. Everything about him was average. He had brown hair and brown eyes. He did have a genuinely nice smile and his teeth were white.

Until she'd met Brown Teeth, she'd never paid much attention to a person's teeth, now she looked at them as an indication of the person's personal hygiene.

"And you, Brandi." Carl didn't immediately let go of Brandi's hand. "If you ever need me to order something special for you, just let me know. I'd be more than happy to."

"Thank you." Brandi removed her hand from his. "I'll do that. For now, Cameron has barely any food in his house."

Carl chuckled. "He usually ate at the café. I don't think he knows how to cook."

"Hey, that's me you're talking about," laughed Cameron. "I can't even deny it because it's true."

"We just ate at The Nugget Café," said Eve. "The food was quite good."

"That's the place Cam always eats," said Carl. "And the food is top notch."

Brandi broke into the conversation. "I need potatoes, carrots and onions."

"Of course, how many of each do you want, Brandi?"

"Four potatoes, eight carrots, and two onions, ought to do it."

"Thank you, Carl." Cameron placed his hand on Eve's waist as he ushered them out. "See you in a bit. Oh, make sure you put all of their purchases on my account. I'm taking them to see Greg and Herb next."

"Sounds, good." Carl smiled at Brandi. "I'll have it ready when you return."

Eve would say Carl was smitten with Brandi, if

the looks he gave her and his handshake was any indication.

The next stop was the butcher, Greg Simmons, a middle-aged man with blond hair and arms the size of tree trunks with hands the size of a ham. But considering his occupation she wasn't surprised he was so big.

Brandi got a four-pound chuck roast. That would provide them with at least two meals, maybe three.

The last stop was the baker, Herb Dunafon. A small man with a balding pate and large, handlebar mustache.

"Hello, ladies, I'm happy to make your acquaintance. I hope you will let me bake something different."

"I'm sorry, Herb," said Eve. "I might be a terrible cook, but I love to bake and I'm good at it. So, until I can bake, we need a loaf of bread, a dozen supper rolls and two dozen sugar cookies, to get by."

Herb gathered the items and put them in a paper bag.

Brandi put the meat on the bottom of the bag and the bread on top.

As they went out the door, Eve looked at Brandi. "Well, that was quite the excursion. I feel like I met everyone in town and it was only three men." Eve smiled. "They certainly seemed to have a special interest in Brandi. Did you notice?"

"That I did," said Cameron, with a grin. "I think it won't be long before we have suitors lining up to take her on an outing."

"Stop it. You two are making a mountain out of a mole hill. They were just trying to be nice," insisted Brandi.

"Nice! I don't think so," said Eve. "I know male interest when I see it, and you do, too."

Brandi rolled her eyes. "Fine. After we leave here, let's go home. I need to start this pot roast so it will be done around seven, a little later than normal for supper, but our lunch was late, too."

They followed Brandi to the mercantile where Carl had put their order on the counter.

Carl was distracted with another customer. Brandi picked up the bag with their vegetables in it, yelled, "Thank you," and hurried out the door.

Outside there seemed to be a gauntlet of men they had to navigate through.

"Hey, Marshal, it's not fair you havin' two gals, and I got none," yelled one man.

"Yeah. That's right." Men started grumbling and some reached for Eve. One man pulled her aside.

"Get your filthy hands off me." Eve elbowed the man in the stomach.

A shot rang out.

The man released her.

Eve pulled herself away and looked behind her.

Cameron stood with his gun out and pointed at the crowd of men. "The next man who touches either of these women, will be a dead man. Do I make myself clear?"

As one, the men backed up and let Eve and Brandi pass.

She held her head high and walked through the group of men, eyeing them. Silently challenging them to try and touch her again.

Eve kept looking back to make sure no one was following them. She'd been in lots of establishments with only men in attendance, but this was the first time she ever felt frightened, even though she didn't show it. What would have happened if Cameron wasn't with them? What would happen when she and Brandi went out on their own?

*C*am walked through the men. "Break it up. Nothing to see now."

The men dispersed except for one. His clothes were worn, but clean. He removed his hat. "Marshal. My name is George Clarendon. I'm the schoolteacher here in Silver City. I met Miss Johnson on the stage here and wondered if I could court her...with her permission, of course."

Cam looked him over. "Met her on the stage, you say?"

"Yes, sir, we took it from Denver together. Well, along with Mrs. Coleman...er, Mrs. Neal."

Cam lifted a brow. "Do I make you nervous, Clarendon?"

"Um...yes, sir, you do." The young man loosened his tie.

"Good. I will ask Brandi if she would like to be courted by you—"

The young man stood straighter. "Excuse me, sir, but wouldn't it be better if I asked Miss Johnson, myself?"

Again, Cam was quiet. He saw the young school-teacher begin to sweat and decided to put him out of his misery. He cocked an eyebrow. "All right. You come by my house in an hour. That will give me time to get home. I won't talk to Brandi, but I *will* see what she says."

Clarendon smiled wide. "Yes, sir. I will. Thank you, sir."

"And, Clarendon, don't call me, sir. I'm either Marshal Neal or Mr. Neal."

"Yes, sir...I mean, Marshal Neal."

"If Brandi says yes, you can call me Cam. Understood?"

"Yes, Marshal Neal. I understand. I'll see you in an hour."

Cam nodded and headed for home. He liked the young schoolteacher but he wondered what Brandi would say.

⸙━━━━━━━━ ━━━ ⸙

$\mathcal{E}$ ve sat at the table an hour or so after they returned home. Brandi had her peeling and cutting carrots for the pot roast.

A knock sounded on the front door.

"Brandi, will you get that, please?" Cam didn't look up from his paper.

"I'll get it." Eve began to rise from the table.

Cam grabbed her hand. "No, I, uh, need to talk to you, privately."

Eve cocked her head and looked at him with her eyebrows furrowed. "All right, Brandi, go ahead and get the door, please."

"Sure." She left the room.

Eve clasped her hands on top of the table. "What did you want to talk to me about?"

Cam smiled and shook his head, then he whispered. "I just wanted Brandi to answer the door. There is a young man, the schoolteacher, who wants to ask if he can court her. He's at the door now."

Eve grinned and then whispered back. "He was very attentive to her on our trip from Denver. I wonder what she'll say?"

"She said, okay." Brandi entered the kitchen and sat at the table. "I probably should have said *no*."

Cam folded his newspaper and put it on the table. "Why? He seems like a nice young man."

Brandi slumped in her chair. "That's just the problem. He is a nice man. What will happen when he finds out I used to be a who—prostitute?"

"He doesn't have to find out," said Eve reasonably.

Brandi shook her head. "I won't do that to him. Sometime someone will come through here who knew me, and I mean in the biblical sense. What will happen then? And what if his student's parents find out? Will they really want their schoolteacher courting a whor...I mean a prostitute?" She crossed her arms on the table and put her head on them. "What have I done?"

Eve went over, sat next to Brandi, and put her arm around her. "You'll hold your head up high. You did what you had to do to survive. No more and no less. If they can't understand that...to heck with them."

"That's easy for you to say, you're married to the marshal. No one's going to say a thing to you about it."

Cam nodded. "That's true they won't, but they won't about you either. You're a part of this family and under my protection."

Brandi lifted her head. "I am? Truly?"

"Of course." Eve smiled at her husband. "You are. You're like my sister and I won't allow anyone to say any different."

Brandi began to cry. "I've never really had a family for a long time. When papa died, I was left with nothing and no way to make a living. Rose found me on the streets and offered me the contract to come work for her. She didn't pull any punches. She told me what I'd be doing but that I'd have a roof over my head and food to eat. She would take half of what I made. That was a better offer than staying on the streets and getting raped and murdered, so I took it. You know the rest."

Cam nodded. "We do and we accept that as a part of your past, but it is your *past*. We all have one. Eve's is being a gambler. That's her past." *I would hate for my sister, Catherine, to be put in such a position. What would she have done to survive had she not married just after father died? She was only sixteen, but she was ready and she was safe. If she didn't have me or marry so early, what would have happened to her?*

Cam nodded. "When is your young man next coming around, Brandi?"

"Tomorrow. I wanted to get my clothes ironed before I go on an outing with him. You do have an iron, don't you?" Brandi lifted her brows a little as she stood.

Cam smiled. "Do you think that just because I was unmarried, I wouldn't have an iron? Well, I do. It's on the floor behind the stove."

"I admit it occurred to me that you would not, especially after finding out you sent your clothes out." Brandi got the iron and set it on the stove to heat. "Where is your ironing board? I saw it but don't remember where."

"In the pantry." He pointed at the door on the same wall as the stove.

"Right." She nodded, retrieved the ironing board, and set it up near the stove. Then she got a dish towel from one of the drawers by the sink, before leaving to get her clothes.

Cam leaned back in his chair. "You did a good thing getting her out of that situation. I admit I'd have done the same thing given that circumstance. And you still need to tell me what they look like."

Eve nodded. She put her elbows on the table and laced her fingers. "Well, Buck is the oldest brother and the one that was shot. He has totally brown teeth. That's what I call him in my head…Brown Teeth. But beyond that he is average height, wiry, not muscular at all, soft with brown hair that reaches his shoulders. He wears a floppy brimmed black hat and has two pearl-handled Colt revolvers.

"The next brother I called Red Bandana because he wears one around his neck. Otherwise, he looks the same as Brown Teeth…er…Buck. He's the younger brother of Brown Teeth, all bones, no muscles at all. He has brown hair and the same kind of hat.

"The one I called Blondie is the youngest brother of Brown Teeth. He's a little taller than the other two and slender, and idolizes his brother, Buck. He's reckless, which is why I say he's the youngest. When you capture them and it's safe for me to go out, I should be able to ply my trade then, right?"

"We're back at the same problem. Just because I know you won't cheat doesn't mean they will accept you and I won't force any saloon owner to let you play."

Eve rested her chin between her palms with her elbows on the table. "Well, heck. What am I supposed to do then?"

CHAPTER SEVEN

"*H*ow about be a wife and help Brandi around here? You know, cleaning and cooking…well, maybe not cooking, since you say you can't cook, but you could learn. Right now we should probably leave the cooking to her."

Eve sat straight. "Yes, I think so because I really don't cook. It wasn't something I learned to do much of growing up. I was more interested in learning to play cards even though Daddy wasn't interested in teaching me…yet. Mama gave up trying to teach me anything, so that was the end of my cooking lessons." She looked up at Brandi. "I will try to learn from you."

Cam covered her hand with his. "I'm sorry you lost your parents."

Eve shrugged, a lump in her throat. "It was a long time ago."

"Still, it hurts. At least it did me. Even though I hated how they fought, I missed them when they were gone."

She nodded. "I suppose. But I came out of it all right. I've been able to support myself, thanks to my father. That's more than Brandi had."

"True." Brandi pulled out a chair from the table and set her wrinkled clothes on it. "But now I have a chance at a new life, and I owe you for that. I'll never be able to repay you for what you did for me."

"I'll never ask you to. Besides, you're paying me back every day by staying here and doing the cooking. You're saving my marriage before it starts."

Cam grinned at Brandi. "That's the truth, because I can't cook either. If it wasn't for the leftovers Blanche always gave me after Sunday supper, I'd have starved."

"We should have Blanche over here for Sunday suppers." Brandi looked at Eve. "After Earl passes, of course."

Eve lifted a brow. "Yes, after he passes." *Which won't be anytime soon, and Brandi knows that fact. I would tell Cameron, but I promised Blanche I would keep her secret...for now. Earl should be miraculously getting better any day now since Cameron and I married.*

Eve looked up at Brandi. "When you're done, I need to iron my clothes, too."

Brandi dipped her chin toward the chair holding her clothes. "Why don't you bring them in here and I'll iron them for you?"

Eve shook her head. "You don't have to do that."

Brandi shrugged. "I'm doing mine. I might as well do yours. I've got supper in the oven and don't have a thing to do until it's ready."

"As long as you're ironing," said Cameron. "I have a couple of shirts that could use a pressing. They don't always do a good job at the Chinese laundry."

"Ah ha. I thought you took your clothes some-where, but now you want *me* to do your laundry." Eve put her hands on her hips. "Brandi's ironing now notwithstanding."

Cameron threw up his hands. "You're my wife. You're supposed to do my laundry, and cook, and clean, and have my babies. That's what wives do."

Eve shot right back at him. "Well, I'm not your average wife. I know I can make a living without you. Most women get married so a man will take care of them. I'm not one of those women." *What if I can't be a good wife after Brandi leaves? And she will leave someday. I need to learn to cook. I can clean and if I have to I can do the laundry, but I can't cook. I don't know how to shop for a meal. What should I do? What can I do? As a wife, I'm definitely lacking.*

"I think I'll leave until the iron gets hot." Brandi stood and practically ran from the kitchen.

"Now see what you've done." Eve pointed after Brandi. "Scared her away."

"I'm not the one yelling like a banshee," said Cameron quietly.

"Well, I'm…" She stopped. "I'm sorry. I shouldn't be yelling. I can talk about this situation like a normal person." She blew out a breath. "I really can. I've just had a long day. Riding in a stagecoach for the last three weeks, getting married and now getting used to my new home. It's a lot for a woman to take in. I'm tired. I'm sure Brandi is, too."

"Well, you can both go to bed early tonight." He stood. "Regardless of how we married or why, I am married and so are you…until death do us part."

She sighed. "I understand that, and I take my vows seriously as well. I wouldn't have married you otherwise. I'm not looking for someone to take care of me. I've been on my own for an awfully long time. I don't intend to suddenly become someone I'm not."

"Why *did* you marry me? You know I won't be able to support you in the lap of luxury because marshals don't make a lot of money. And I'd bet it wasn't just because the Stone brothers are after you. What was the real reason?"

She sighed. "You want to know the truth?"

"I wouldn't have asked if I didn't want the truth."

"Very well. I'm tired of moving on to the next town, of only having a room above the saloon or in a hotel and nothing I can call my own. I want a family, Cameron. I want children and stability. I figured being married to the marshal can give me that. I'll hang my red dress up…for now. And I'll try to be a good wife to you."

"Why were you so adamant to continue playing poker if you're tired of it?"

"I didn't say I was tired of poker. I'm tired of constantly moving around. And because the thought of being beholden to anyone for my survival scares me. But I'm willing to try."

"Thank you. I'll try to be a good husband."

She leaned forward and grinned. "I know where to find another one if you aren't."

Cameron threw his head back and laughed. "You think any of those men we saw today will be a better husband. They won't give you a choice about sleeping arrangements any more than I am, but they also won't give you a choice about having sex. I will. I understand you won't want to tonight, that you're tired, but I also won't wait forever. You want children and so do I. We both know what we must do to create a child."

Eve nodded. "I know. Johnny and I were married for two years and I never got pregnant. I may not be able to for all I know," she said softly, her head down. "Or he might not have been able to father a child. Or maybe we were just unlucky. What will you do with me if I can't give you children?"

Cameron lifted a brow and reached for her hand.

She let him hold it.

"I won't abandon you. We'll figure out another way to have children. We'll adopt or give a home to an abandon child. They run the streets here but won't let me get close. They're afraid I'll throw them in jail."

Eve frowned. "Who has been filling their head with that nonsense? It is nonsense, isn't it?" He continued to hold her hand. *Does he know he's still holding my hand, or is he just comfortable doing so?*

He released her hand and shrugged. "Yes. I would never put a child in jail. And I don't know who might be telling them I will. I wish I knew who to talk to. I'd make it clear that I only want to help. I have no desire to have a jail full of unwanted children. Even if I did, with a population approaching two thousand people, my jail is normally full of drunks, if no one else." Cameron stood and paced from the table to the sink and back. "I think some of the kids are just out there because their parents can't afford to keep them anymore. The little ones are the ones I feel sorriest for. I'll bet you some of those kids aren't more than four or five. But even they won't let me near. If I get too close, an older child will run between us and the little one runs away."

Her heart hurt when she thought of those children out there, alone and probably hungry. "Cameron, there has got to be something we can do. I hate to see children forsaken and left to the streets."

"So do I. We'll talk about it more later. Now, you should unpack."

"Would you like to come with me? I have another question for you."

"Right behind you." When they were in the hall-way, he asked, "Why do you call me Cameron? Everyone else calls me Cam."

Eve made her way to their bedroom and found her bags. She turned and faced him.

"Is that what you want me to call you? I like Cameron. Cam seems disrespectful for some reason."

He smiled. "Only my mother ever called me Cameron. I think I'd like it if you want to call me that."

"I do. It's more dignified."

"Then Cameron it is."

Eve placed her bags on the bed and opened one. It contained her skirts and blouses. Two black bombazine skirts which should last her nearly forever and one blue-and-white striped skirt, which was slightly dressier. Her three plain blouses in blue, pink and white were also in the bag. She took the clothes out and laid them on the bed.

The second carpetbag contained three dresses, including her red silk dress, two corsets, three pair of bloomers, one pair of black shoes and six pair of stockings with garters. It also contained most of her money sewn into the lining.

"Cameron, do you have a knife or a pair of scissors I could use?"

"I have both, which do you prefer?"

"The scissors, please."

He walked over to the tallboy dresser, bent down, and opened the bottom drawer. He returned with a sewing kit stocked with scissors, needles, thread, thimbles, and straight pins.

"You are well prepared," she commented.

"I've been a bachelor for a long time. I need to know how to do some things myself. I don't want to take a shirt to the laundry every time I lose a button."

"Smart man." She got to work cutting the stitches holding the lining. Then she removed the money and put it on the bed next to her. By the time she was done there was approximately one thousand dollars on the bed.

"Whooweee! That's a lot of money. If you had this much money, why become a mail-order bride?"

"I guess what it really comes down to is I was

ready to settle down and have a home I could call my own."

"You could have bought a little house and lived for quite a while on that money."

"Yes, but then what? I'd have to go back to wearing my red dress and back into the smoky saloons to gamble and make money to live on. Plus, I'm tired of living alone."

Cameron picked up the red dress from the bed. "This red dress?"

"Yes. As you can see, it leaves little to the imagination."

He straightened the garment as he laid it back on the bed. "I understand that feeling. I'm thirty-three years old and feel like it's time to settle down. I admit, your beauty swayed me."

"As did your handsome face. So, we both admit to being drawn to each other by our appearance. Not exactly the best things to base a marriage on, but there you have it. We're both shallow people after all." She straightened and looked around the room. "Where can I put this money?"

He ran a hand behind his neck. "I think you should put it in the bank."

Eve shook her head. Her frustration at the situation filled her. *It was her money. Hers!* "If I put it in the bank, I must have you with me to take any out, because it would technically be your money. I want immediate access to it. Whenever I want it. It's my money. I earned it, every last dollar and it took me a long time to accumulate it."

He reached for her. "I can always come with you. I don't want your money, Eve."

She backed away and stood apart, not wanting his touch. Not wanting him to persuade her to do things his way. "Good, then you won't mind if I don't put it in the bank. And what if we have a fight and I want to leave, would you still be available to come with me to close my account?"

He was silent for a moment and looked down at his hands, resting in his lap. "How can you say you'll leave, if you take your vows seriously?"

Eve studied his face, opened her mouth to refute what he said and then closed it again. Finally, she gazed directly at him. "Just because I believe in my vows, doesn't mean I will live in a bad marriage. No thank you. I'll find a place here in the house to put it." She stopped and gazed over at him. "Besides, don't take this the wrong way, but if something should happen and we need the money, it's available."

He sat on the bed. "If that's your wish. But even if you have it here, I won't let you go, just because we have a fight. We need to stay together and work it out. We can't give up at the first sign of trouble."

She finished emptying the carpetbags and set them in the bottom of the closet. "I know that, and I would only leave out of great necessity. If there is no way we can settle our differences, then I would leave, because I'd rather not be married if that is the case."

"I understand. I wouldn't either. I've seen first-hand how damaging that can be, not only to the participants in the marriage but to any children. I admit I was affected by my parents fighting. I would rather divorce than go through what they did."

"I don't blame you. I feel the same way." She changed the subject, feeling like they were being too melancholy. "You have an exceedingly small closet for two people. We'll have to find a different place for the bags without the money. They take up too much room. My dresses would be wrinkled in no time if we leave them there. Do you have a barn or a shed?"

He nodded. "I have a barn for my horse. There's plenty of room in there."

"Good." She looked at the floor. "And thank you for marrying me. I know now you didn't have to."

Cameron stood and took Eve's hands in his. "I honestly believe we can make a go of this if we try. I know working together could be difficult, but I think we can do it. We're two smart people. We can figure it out, whatever *it* is."

"I believe you're right." She extricated her hands from his. "But we need ground rules. Like there will be no physical punishment. The first time you hit me in anger, I'll leave. I won't be used as a punching bag."

His jaw clenched and his eyes narrowed. "I'll never hit you. Period. If by chance I do, you have my permission to shoot me. I do ask that you don't kill me, just wound me."

She smiled and then stared at him for a moment. "You're serious."

He didn't smile. "As a minister on Sunday."

"Well, that stance is somewhat reassuring, if a bit unusual."

"I want you to know you are safe with me. I believe we can build a good marriage, if we try, and that's all I'm asking…that we both put our best foot forward and try."

"You make a good argument, and I'll consider it. I have to tell you, though, I originally thought of this marriage as just a way to lie low for a while until the Stone brothers stopped looking for me."

"Do you believe that? That they will stop looking for you." He shook his head. "In all my years as a law enforcement officer, I've never seen thieves or murderers give up."

She slumped onto the bed, resting her elbows on her knees. "I believed it until just this minute. Shall we finish this conversation in the kitchen? Brandi needs to know why you think this way, too."

"Certainly." He waved an arm at the door. "After you."

Eve picked up her clothes and led the way to the kitchen.

When they entered, Brandi was in the process of ironing her clothes. Eve put her clothes on the chair with Brandi's. "Here you go. Are you sure you want to iron them? I do know how, believe it or not, it's one of the things Mama did manage to get through my head. She told me, no matter what I did, I'd want to keep my clothes up because I might not be able to afford to replace them. So, I learned." She looked over at Cameron and lifted a brow. "I even know how to do laundry, if I have to."

Cameron laughed. "I thought you said you didn't know how."

Eve smiled. "That was before we had our little tete-a-tete."

Brandi set the iron back on the stove. "I'll do them. I don't have anything else to do and I do want to look my best for tomorrow, and the next day and the next. I'm sure you do, too."

Eve got herself a mug and held it up for Cameron to see.

He nodded. "Yes, please."

"How about you, Brandi? Want a cup of coffee? And to take a break for a minute?"

"Sure. What's up?"

Eve got another cup and walked to the table holding the cups in one hand and the coffeepot in the other. She set a cup in front of each of them and where she would be sitting. Then she filled each and returned the pot to the stove.

Cameron jutted his chin toward the door next to the stove. "Sorry there's no cream but we have sugar in the pantry, if you need some."

Eve shook her head. "I'll take mine black. I'm learning to like it. Not every place has cream and sugar so I'm trying not to need them to enjoy the coffee."

"I like mine black, too," said Brandi, who then took a sip. "Grew up without milk or sugar, so I didn't have a choice."

"Now, you were saying about the Stone brothers." Eve gazed at Cameron.

---

*B*uck Stone and his brothers were on Eve's trail. They'd followed her to Denver and then checked the stage office to see where she went. The stage master had needed just a little persuading and Buck was more than happy to hold him at gunpoint.

The man said a woman who looked like Eve along with another woman with red hair and covered in bruises, had bought tickets to Silver City in the Nevada Territory.

"How long to get there?" Buck kept his gun aimed at the sweating man.

"About tw…two weeks," said the short balding man. His mustache caught the sweat as it ran down his face.

"Thanks for the information," said Buck. "Now turn around."

That man did.

Buck hit him on the back of the head.

The stage master fell to the floor.

"That ought to give you a good excuse for giving me the information, in case anyone asks. Besides, it was fun."

Buck grinned as he left the office and mounted. "We're headed to Silver City, in the Nevada Territory." He turned his horse and headed west. The time wouldn't be long now before he found both those bitches and taught them each a lesson. Nobody steals from Buck Stone.

CHAPTER EIGHT

*E*ve watched the frown form on Brandi's beautiful face.

"What about those…devils?" asked Brandi.

Cameron swallowed a sip of coffee and set his cup on the table. "They won't stop looking for you. Period. Eve said she thought she would just stay here for a while until they stopped looking, but in my experience, they won't stop looking. Ever." He looked at Eve. "Based on what you've said, you not only took their money but you, your friend actually, shot the oldest brother and embarrassed them. Wounded their pride." He shook his head. "They'll never stop. You're safest here where I can protect you."

"Can you guarantee you can protect us?" asked Brandi.

"Good question," said Eve. "Can you?"

"No. I can't guarantee it, and I'd be lying if I said I could." He took a deep breath and then released it slowly. "But I can promise that I and my deputies will do our best."

"How many deputies do you have?" asked Eve.

"Three. Silver City is growing and for every two or three thousand new people I need an additional deputy. I have three deputies, Robert E. Lee, no relation to the Confederate general, Sam Chism, and Jake LeRoy. If you need anything when I'm not around, you can tell them, and they will find me."

"That's good to know. I hope you introduce Brandi and me to them soon."

Cameron looked at Brandi. "Would you feel comfortable having them over for supper? Robert is newly married. His wife's name is Mcthabel. Sam is a bachelor and Jake is a widower with a teenaged daughter. That would be an extra five people, or we can have them separately. That might be the best since I'd have to get extra chairs otherwise."

Brandi put her elbows on the table and rested her chin on her hand. Then she sat up. "Yes, I believe the small groups would be better. Also, I'm not saying it will happen, but if George and I hit it off, I'd like to invite him to supper sometimes, too."

Eve nodded. "I think that's a fine idea. How about you, Cameron?"

He shrugged. "That's fine with me. As long as you're doing the cooking, and you keep it as inexpensive as you can, you can invite whomever you like."

The smile Brandi gave him was brilliant.

Eve watched the two of them and chuckled. "Well, now that we have that out of the way, when is supper?"

Brandi laughed. "She gets close to real food and she can't wait to eat. That didn't ever happen after the first stop for food on the stagecoach. The stuff, beans and stale bread was so horrible, we only ate about once every three days. You'd have thought that at least one time they would have offered fresh beans and just-baked bread, but no, not once in thirty days on the stagecoach. I don't know how those drivers do it. They're a hearty group of men, I can tell you that."

Eve snapped her fingers for attention. "Regardless, the question stands. When will supper be ready? I can iron if you need to stop to get it on the table."

Brandi laughed and placed the iron on the back of the stove so it wouldn't get too hot. "It's all right. Supper's ready and we can eat any time."

Eve's stomach rumbled and she covered it with her hands. "And you didn't say anything before now?" Her voice rose on the last word.

Brandi grinned and she looked over at Cameron. "She's always like this unless you take her out to eat. Then she has the best manners I've ever seen."

Eve's face heated under Brandi's praise. She never thought of her behavior as good manners so much as just being polite. If she didn't know Brandi so well, she would never have questioned her on the lateness of her announcement about supper.

"I'm just hungry, that's all. And I've spent too many days with an empty belly to pass up good food."

Cameron cocked an eyebrow. "How can you be so hungry when it's only been about five hours since we ate at the café?"

"Trust me, five hours is a long time between good meals."

"You don't know that the meal will be good. You just have my word." Brandi lifted a brow and leaned on her hand while her elbow rested on the table.

"I'll take your word any day because I know you." Eve turned toward Cameron. "Haven't you anything to say?"

"Nothing, and I wouldn't want to get in the middle of that conversation anyway. However, if you ladies would like, I'll set the table, since one of us doesn't have any idea of what's where in here."

Eve chuckled. "I'll follow and make note of everything. Then I can, at least, help that much with meals. I can make bread and several different types of cookies, and I make a decent pie crust, so I can bake pies. I'm not totally useless. I just can't cook. You set a pot roast, like we're having today, in front of me, and I haven't any idea what to do with it."

Brandi came around and hugged her. "It's okay. I'll cook and you can bake since I don't do that very well."

Cameron laughed. "Looks like, between the two of you I got a pretty good wife."

Eve looked for something to throw at him but came up empty. "You'll get yours, Cameron Neal. I don't know what yet, but I'll get you back for saying such a thing. Brandi didn't marry you, and someday she'll get married and settle down to have babies of her own. What will we do then?"

He leaned forward resting his forearms on the table. "What will we do? I don't know." He lifted a brow. "Maybe you could learn to cook."

"Or you could hire a cook."

"Not on a marshal's wage we can't."

"We could if I went back to gambling."

Cameron's lips flattened into a straight line.

He was angry and Eve didn't care. She would not be the only one changing in this relationship. *I know I really don't want to play cards anymore, but I'll be darned if I have to give them up and have to learn to cook, too, while he does nothing.*

"Or." Brandi laid her hand on Eve's shoulder and interrupted the bickering. "I could never leave. I don't see myself getting married. I can't imagine a man will want to marry me after he learns about my background."

Eve reached up and covered her hand with one of hers. "You'll just have to wait until the right man comes along. He won't care about your past. It's past. Everyone has one. Don't let yours rob you of your happiness. Promise me." She looked up at Brandi. "Promise me."

"I promise. But that man will have to be incredibly special, indeed. Now let's get supper on the table. Eve's not the only one who's hungry."

Is Brandi right? Am I giving her a false sense of security by believing that there is a man out there who will accept her despite her past?

---

*A*fter supper, Eve did the dishes. Brandi finished the ironing.

Cameron went to the living room to read his paper. When he was done, he came back into the kitchen retrieved a cup and poured himself a cup of coffee before sitting at the table.

Brandi yawned. "I'm tired. It's been a long day, and I'm going to bed. I have to finish putting my things away now, anyway."

"It has been a full day." Cameron agreed. "I believe it is bedtime. Morning comes early."

Eve looked at both of them. "You're right, I suppose. Good night, Brandi. See you in the morning."

On her way out of the kitchen, Brandi waved. "Good night, you two."

"Good night, Brandi." Cameron stood and turned to Eve. "After you, wife."

Eve rolled her eyes. "As you wish, husband."

He sighed. "What I wish and what will happen are two entirely different things."

Eve laughed. "You're right about that." She walked to their bedroom. Once there she started to prepare for bed by taking down her hair. Putting it up in a bun while wet left soft waves in it. She liked them and the way they cascaded over her shoulders down to her waist. Eve liked her hair, was proud of it and sometimes she braided it, sometimes not. Tonight, she didn't think she would.

Then she unbuttoned her blouse and stopped before removing it. "Would you turn around please?"

"Why? We're married."

"That may be but I've lived alone for a long time and I'm not ready to share my body with you, so please turn your back to me."

He turned.

She removed her blouse, folded it over one of the chairs, followed by her skirt. She took her flannel nightgown off the bed and put it on. Then she put the rest of her things on top of the bureau until she could clean out a drawer for them.

"You can turn back now."

When he faced her again, he waved his arm up and down in front of her. "Won't you be more comfortable without all that?"

"Maybe, but for tonight I'm wearing all of it. I want to make sure we don't forget our agreement and make love tonight. I'm really not ready to take that step."

Cameron stood by the side of the bed having removed his shirt. "All right but know this, Eve, I'll never take you against your will."

"That's good to know."

He sat and took off his boots and then his pants.

Eve couldn't help but look. Her new husband was a fine-looking man. Lean, with well-defined muscles, she found herself wondering what it would be like to be made love to by him.

※

*M*orning came with the sunrise shining through the window and Eve cuddled next to Cameron.

Good grief, what am I doing? Her stomach was suddenly filled with butterflies. She was as nervous as an untried schoolgirl.

"Good morning."

His voice rumbled through his chest and into her.

"Good morning."

He lifted his arm.

She scooted away.

"I'm sorry. I must have gotten cold."

"That's fine. More than fine, actually. I like waking with my wife in my arms."

"Regardless, I'll try not to let it happen again."

He chuckled. "Oh, it will happen again, Eve. Mark my words."

She huffed out a breath. "We'll see about that." Eve got out of bed and, keeping her back to him, put on the same clothes she had on yesterday. No sense in changing just to do housework.

When she was dressed, she hurried out of the room. She heard his laughter as she shut the door.

When she got to the kitchen, she lit the stove and heated the coffee from yesterday. She didn't throw out what was still good because coffee was precious.

"Good morning." Brandi came in yawning but fully dressed. "Oh, good, you put on the coffee. We'll have leftovers tonight."

Cameron walked in and got himself a cup of coffee. "That sounds great. You two are in for a treat when we go to Earl and Blanche's for supper."

"If her meals are anything like her pie, I'm all in." Eve chuckled at her gambling reference.

"Gambling metaphors abound with you don't they?" asked Cameron.

Eve shrugged. "I suppose they do. I never really thought about it. I suppose the metaphors depend on what you do in life."

"You don't want to know what I usually say," said Brandi. "I can curse with the best of them. But I'm trying really hard to remember what I learned in school. I did go to school, you know. I'm not totally ignorant."

"Honey," said Eve. "I never thought you were. You're probably the most well-spoken prostitute I know."

Brandi laughed. "I'm the only prostitute you know. Former prostitute."

Eve smiled and her face heated to pinpoints in her cheeks. "Well, there is that."

Cameron laughed.

So did Brandi.

Eve finally chuckled and then laughed. "If we start out every day with a good laugh, we'll have a great day, wait and see. Although, getting up this early is hard for someone like me. I suppose the journey here was of use in that department. It broke me of the habit of staying up most of the night and sleeping most of the day. Instead we stayed up all night and all day."

Brandi stood. "I'll make breakfast. I hope scrambled eggs and toasted bread are all right with everyone because that's all we have. Once we go to the mercantile and the butcher, we'll have more choices. I guess we're lucky we aren't having pot roast for breakfast."

"Hey, I wouldn't mind at all," said Cameron. "That was a great meal we had last night."

Brandi blushed under his praise.

Eve smiled. Brandi was coming into her own and feeling surer of herself. That made Eve happy.

Now if she could be as content herself. But she wondered what her marriage would bring. Would she have children? Could she have children? She hadn't with Johnny. Maybe they were just unlucky like she'd told Cameron, but she was also afraid she couldn't and that would break her heart.

CHAPTER NINE

*E*ve dressed with care, wearing her light blue blouse and the blue-and-white striped skirt. She wanted to make a good impression on Cameron's deputy and his wife.

She checked herself in the mirror on the bureau. *I'll have to see about getting a cheval mirror. I wonder if I could get one from San Francisco that wouldn't get broken on the way here?*

Robert and Methabel Lee arrived at six o'clock on the dot.

Eve joined Cameron at the door.

"Robert, glad you could make it." Cameron extended his hand.

Robert shook it.

"And Methabel, lovely as ever." Cameron put his arm around Eve's waist hugging her a little closer.

"This is my wife Eve. Our friend, Brandi, is in the kitchen finishing supper."

Eve put out her hand. "Pleased to meet you, Robert."

Robert shook her hand. "Pleased to meet you, too, Eve."

Methabel seemed noticeably young and shy. Eve would have bet she wasn't more than sixteen or seventeen.

"Please to meet you, too, Methabel." Eve extended her hand toward the girl.

"You, too, Mrs. Neal."

"Call me, Eve. We don't stand on ceremony in this house." She turned toward her husband. "Do we, dear?"

"No, we don't, m'dear."

"Let me take your lovely shawl," Eve said to Methabel.

She took off her shawl, knitted in various shades of blue, and handed it to Eve. She was a pretty girl, blonde with blue eyes and if Eve wasn't mistaken, she was expecting, too or the green calico dress she wore was hideously cut.

Robert was also younger than Eve would have suspected, probably mid-twenties, with sandy blonde hair and deep blue eyes.

They would have beautiful children.

"Cameron tells me you two are newly married. Is

that right?"

Robert began to laugh. "Cam has no sense of time. We were married almost a year ago. Methabel is already six months along."

Eve released a deep breath. "Oh, thank goodness. I was afraid to say anything. How are you doing? Is Robert treating you well?"

"Oh, yes, ma'am." Methabel looked up at her husband. "Robbie spoils me really. He helps me with the dishes every night so we can go to bed early. He knows how I need my rest."

Eve covered her mouth with her fingers to hide her smile. "It's nice he's so thoughtful."

"Oh, yes, Robbie is very thoughtful."

Cameron put his hand at Eve's waist. "Shall we move into the kitchen and you can meet our friend, Brandi?"

"Of course," said Robert.

Eve walked in first followed by Methabel, then Robbie and then Cameron.

Suddenly there was the sound of glass shattering.

Eve looked up and saw Brandi wide-eyed, staring at Robert.

"Oh, clumsy me. I'll just get the broom and clean this up." Brandi retrieved the broom from the back porch and cleaned up the mess. Then she rinsed her hands in the basin at the sink before coming forward.

"Hi, I'm Brandi." She held out her hand to

Methabel.

"I'm Methabel and this is my husband, Robbie."

Brandi extended her hand to Robert. "Pleased to meet you…Robbie."

The man blushed clear to his ears. "And you, too…ma'am."

She waved him away. "Please, Brandi will do."

Eve watched how Brandi and Robert kept their eyes on each other and wondered if Methabel saw it, too. She looked down at the girl, who was quite petite, like Brandi. As a matter of fact, if Brandi had been a blonde instead of a redhead, they could have been twins. Interesting.

"Supper is ready. If you all will sit, I'll bring it to the table." Brandi moved toward the stove.

"Here, let me help." Eve got the mashed potatoes and gravy.

Brandi brought over the pork roast along with a carving knife and set it in front of Cameron. "Would you carve please?"

"Certainly," said Cameron.

She gave him the carving knife and a large fork.

Eve's mouth watered at the heavenly smells coming from the food. Her stomach rumbled.

Everyone chuckled.

Eve shrugged her shoulders. "I can't help it. Good food always makes me even hungrier."

Once everyone was seated—Cameron at the head

of the table, Robert and Methabel to his left and Eve and Brandi to his right—the meal began.

Everyone passed their plates to Cameron for a slice of the roast, then the potatoes, gravy, green beans cooked with bacon, and carrots glazed in honey, were passed around the table.

After a few minutes, Eve looked at Methabel. "So, Methabel, where did you and Robert meet?"

"We met at the mercantile." She looked over and reached for her husband's hand, placing their clasped hands on the table. "My daddy has a ranch about fifteen miles east of town. He supplies beef to the butcher and horses for the pony express riders and the stagecoach company. We come into town every Saturday and Robert saw me and went to my daddy and asked if he could court me. Daddy said yes, I think because Robbie asked him before he asked me."

"Interesting," said Brandi. "The man courting me did the same thing. He asked Cameron before he asked me. I suppose we wouldn't be hurt then, if they said, no."

Methabel nodded. "I'm sure you're right."

"Clarendon is a good man—that's the man courting Brandi." Cameron forked a bit of meat. "He's the schoolteacher here in town."

"George Clarendon?" asked Robert. "I know him and Brandi couldn't find a better man."

"He's been teaching here for about five years,"

said Methabel. "He was the man who graduated me from school. I was the only one in my class. Everyone else was younger than I was."

"When did you graduate?" Eve couldn't help herself asking the question.

Methabel smiled. "Last year. I met Robbie just after that. I know I look young but I'm eighteen now, I was nearly an old maid. All my friends were already married and had kids by that time. That's why I was the only one in my class."

"Of course. I understand completely," said Eve.

Brandi looked at Robert. "And Robbie, you came here from Ft. Worth if I understood correctly. Did you go to work for Cameron right away?"

Robert's gaze never left Brandi's. "No, I came up here to make my fortune and like ninety percent of the men here, I didn't make it. Most of them continue digging and making enough to eek out a living, but not me. I wanted more than that. Cameron found me and hired me and mentored me. I can't ever repay him for the kindness he showed me." Finally he turned his gaze onto his wife. "I wouldn't have my wife or soon my child if not for Cam."

Eve's eyes teared up, hearing what kind of man her husband was. "Sounds like I got very lucky with my husband."

Cameron laughed. "I've been telling her I'm the best one there is."

They all laughed and finished their meal.

Eve was sure her suspicions were correct. Brandi and Robert knew each other…in the Biblical sense.

After supper while Eve and Brandi did the dishes, she sent the rest of them into the living room. "Tell me you didn't know him from Ft. Worth." Eve whispered to Brandi.

She shook her head and looked toward the living room. "I can't because I did. He was one of my best customers and the only one that I came close to giving my heart to. And he was the only one who bathed before he came to see me."

"Are you afraid he'll give away your secret?" Eve wiped a plate dry and put it in the cupboard before grabbing another dish from the hot water.

Brandi put another plate in the bucket with the rinse water. "No, it would give his away, too. I can't imagine his bride would be happy to know he visited a prostitute on a regular basis." She washed several pieces of silverware and tossed them in the bucket with the hot rinse water.

Eve shook her head. "No, I don't suppose she would. Well, let's forget it and take coffee out to everyone. If you get the cups, I'll get the pot."

Together they went out and served the coffee. Visited a while longer and then the Lees said goodnight.

After Cameron closed the door behind them, he

turned to Eve and Brandi. "Tell me what I don't know. You two made eyes at each other all night."

"You might as well sit down," said Brandi. When he had, she continued. "I used to know Robert... Robbie...when I was a prostitute. He was a regular customer. I'm sure he won't say anything about it, and I certainly won't. I have no desire to wreck his marriage. She seems like a nice girl, and he deserves to be with someone nice."

"Were you in love with him?" asked Eve as gently as she could.

"No," Brandi shook her head. "Not really. We knew nothing could come of it but we were both lonely and so we became lovers mostly on my day off when he didn't have to pay. He was real poor then."

"Yes, I know," said Cameron. "I took him in when he first came here. I saw him begging on the street and because he was young and I thought I saw promise in him, I took him in. He's become one heck of a deputy in the last three years. I'd hate for anything to happen to tarnish that."

With her eyes narrowed Brandi looked straight at Cameron. "So, would I. Nothing makes me happier than to see Robert succeeding. I won't jeopardize that."

"Just so we understand one another."

Brandi kept staring at Cameron. "I know you don't know me, but you'll have to trust me on this matter. I won't bring shame to this family, assuming you still want me as part of your family."

Cameron rolled his eyes and ran a hand through his hair. "Of course, I want you to be a part of this family. You and Eve are sisters for all intents and purposes. I wouldn't change that connection for all the world."

Brandi's smile lit up the room. "Good. I've never had a sister or a brother before. I like it and don't want to lose the feeling I have in my heart. I feel warm all over."

Eve smiled. "I feel that way, too. I think it comes from having a home and people who care about you." She looked at Cameron. "I know you probably don't feel like that yet, since you've always had a home, but you will feel it as you get used family. The more you get to know us, the more you'll like us, I guarantee it."

He grinned. "I already appreciate you both. Especially Brandi." He looked at Eve. "You never told me she was such a great cook, just that she could cook."

Eve widened her eyes. "I didn't know either. She'd never cooked for me before." *Should I be afraid because he appreciates Brandi's skills, especially since I don't appear to have any?*

"Well, I'd say we all have something to be thankful for, tonight. And on that note, I'm going to bed." Brandi stood and left the living room.

"I think I'll join her," said Eve. "Are you coming?"

"Right behind you, after I lock up. This is a mining town with lots of people down on their luck because they didn't make the big strike. They'll do anything for money to eat, drink or gamble, so even when you're here by yourselves, you should lock the doors and windows. I know that's hard to do when it's stifling hot but you should still consider it."

"I usually carry my derringer in my pocket. I didn't yesterday or today because I thought we were safe, but I'll start carrying it again. And if you'll give me the keys I'll have more made so Brandi and I can each have a set of keys to the house."

He nodded. "That's a good idea. I'll see you shortly…and Eve?"

She cocked her head a bit to the side. "Yes?"

"Don't wear your nightgown or underthings tonight. I want us to start getting to know each other."

"What do you mean *know*?"

"I don't mean make love, we'll wait on that for a while, but I won't wait forever, either."

"I don't expect you to. I know I seem to be acting the virgin and I'm most certainly not, but I just want to be with you for more than two nights."

"Just so we're clear."

"Right. Clear as mud." She sauntered off toward their bedroom.

CHAPTER TEN

a single lamp on her bedside table threw the room into shadow, but Eve saw Cameron clearly when he entered. Eve was already under the covers with them tucked tightly under her arms. Her shoulders were visible, but no more so than when she wore her red dress.

"I see you followed my instructions."

She pursed her lips. "I prefer to think of them as suggestions because if they were instructions, I'd still be in my nightgown. I don't take well to being told what to do."

He chuckled. "Whatever makes you happy." He proceeded to undress.

Eve blatantly watched him, again admiring his physique. Again, wondering what making love with him would be like.

126

When Cameron sat to remove his boots, the bed dipped. "What are you thinking about so intently?"

"I was thinking about my dead husband. He was a terrible lover. Even I knew that, and I was a virgin. I just wonder what the woman he was in bed with when he died, saw in him. His youth, maybe. She was about twenty years older than he was, and I don't know what he saw in her. Whatever it was cost them both their lives."

"I'm sorry you had such a bad first marriage. That would certainly put me off marriage and the marital bed but I promise to take care of you when we make love. I won't hurt you and hopefully you'll feel only pleasure."

She turned toward him and propped up on one elbow. "If I don't feel that way, what then?"

"Then we have to work together to make it better." He stood and took off his pants, followed by his drawers, leaving them both where they laid on the floor. Then he got under the blankets and turned toward her propping himself up on an elbow like she was.

"What now, Cameron?"

"Well, for what I had in mind, we need to be closer together. I want us to touch each other and learn each other's bodies."

"Why? That seems like an odd thing to do. All you need to do is rutt on me and we'll be done."

Cameron closed his eyes and clenched his jaw. "I swear if your husband wasn't already dead, I'd shoot him now for the way he treated you." He closed his eyes for a moment, then opened them and looked at her. "Let me show you how you should be treated." Then he reached over and touched her right arm, running his fingers up and down her arm with a feather light touch. "We can learn where the other likes to be touched and where we don't. Then when we finally do make love we'll be ahead of the game and able to enjoy the act of making love much more."

"All right, I do like the way you rubbing my arm makes me feel."

"You can touch me, too, if you like."

She nodded, scooted closer and began exploring his body. Her hand was pale against his tanned skin as she moved through the sparse, curly dark hair that wrapped around her fingers as she slowly walked them over his chest.

Eve eased her fingers up his neck, the shadow of whiskers on his chin scraped against her. His lips were firm and yet she knew them to be soft against her lips.

Touching him was highly stimulating. Seeing his reaction to her touch gave her information she tucked away for use later.

Then it was his turn and she was surprised at how gentle he was with her. She felt things with him she never did with Johnny. Good feelings and yet feelings of need.

She knew he needed more but he stopped and held out his arm. "Come over here. You'll end up here anyway, so you might as well start here."

She laughed and scooted over. Curling into him and covering his chest with her arm, she let her palms glide over the same hair she'd just explored with her fingers. "Men are so different from women. Where you're hard, I'm soft and vice versa. We fit together so well. Johnny and I never cuddled like this. He would just have sex with me and then roll over and go to sleep. He never cared enough to find out where I like to be touched or how. I don't have anyone to compare you to because you are so different from what I've known before."

"I've never known a woman like you. You're exceptionally beautiful and obviously smart but in some ways very naïve. I still can't believe you're my wife. I'll thank Earl for finding you for me for the rest of my life."

"You'll be able to thank him on Sunday. Maybe he'll be feeling better by then." A stab of guilt came along with the words. She hated keeping this from Cameron. She knew he would soon find out about her duplicity and she doubted he would take it well.

"I don't think so." Cameron lay back and tightened his hold on her while he put his other arm over his head and stared at the ceiling. He let out a long breath before he spoke, his voice barely more than a whisper. "He's been going downhill for a couple of months now."

"Really? A couple of months, you say?" She closed her eyes and wanted to curse Earl and Blanche for what they put Cameron through.

"Yeah. It's been sad to watch."

"Well, you never know what can happen. Now that you're settled, maybe he'll start to recover. Maybe it was his worry for you that had him sick." Earl had better be a lot better or she'd be having words with the old man.

"I'd hate to be the cause, but if he gets better now, I don't care. I just want him well."

"I'm sure he will be. Give him time." She patted his chest. Eve hated to lie to him, but the truth would do no one any good, so a white lie wouldn't hurt him or his relationship with his godparents. "I feel like I can sleep now. How about you?"

Cameron looked down at her and smiled. "I'm afraid I won't be sleeping for a while."

She chuckled. "You won't always have that problem. Don't think about what we aren't doing, but what we are. Lying together and learning to be close without having to make love. For now, give me a couple more days. I know I'm not a virgin and you probably think I'm acting like one, but I've never been with any man but my dead husband. I need some time to get used to the idea."

He rubbed her back slowly, up and down.

Eve found it hard to keep her eyes open and then decided *why fight it*? She closed her eyes and tried to go to sleep but she kept seeing Cameron's anger when he found out about Earl. Sleep would be a long time coming.

*C*ameron watched his wife sleep and held her in his arms like that was where she was always supposed to be. Was this feeling why he'd never married? Was he meant to wait for Eve? She did seem perfect for him, if not for the gambling, but she'd agreed to stop. He'd have to make sure she didn't want to go back. Perhaps when she got with child, she wouldn't have the desire any longer. Perhaps.

*T*he following day began over coffee and laughing about how awful they all looked in the morning.

Eve laughed when Cameron entered the kitchen.

"You look like you were doing headstands in your pillow."

He came over to the sink where she was filling a bucket with water and wrapped his arms around her. "And you dear wife, look like you slept in a windstorm." He moved her hair with one hand and kissed her on the neck.

Eve decided last night while she was lying in Cameron's arms, they'd make love tonight, if he still wanted to. She didn't really think he'd say no, but she just never knew how a man would react.

She looked over at Brandi who was cooking breakfast.

Brandi smiled, shook her head, and rolled her eyes before turning back to the stove.

After breakfast Cameron stood and headed to the door. But he stopped, pulled Eve up from the table and into his arms. He kissed her so hard she was dizzy when they finally came up for air. "What was that for?"

"If something should happen to me, I want our last kiss to be one you remember."

She placed a palm on her chest to slow the beating of her heart and control her racing pulse. "Well, you certainly made it hard to forget."

He laughed. "Then I've done my job well." He went out the door.

Eve was still touching her lips when Brandi came back into the kitchen.

Brandi sat at the table. "What did I miss?"

"What makes you think you missed something?" Eve dropped her hand and put it behind her back.

"Well, it could be the way you were standing there touching your lips like you've never been kissed before."

Eve smiled and lifted the bucket from the sink and took it to the stove. She placed it on a hot burner to heat. "I feel like I never *have* been kissed before. That kiss was amazing."

Brandi laughed. "You're so funny. I figure I've kissed hundreds of men over the years, and yet, I don't think I've ever had one whose kiss left me speechless." She quieted. "The closest I ever came was…Robert. That man knew how to kiss. His wife is a lucky woman."

Eve sat across the table from Brandi. "You'll have your special man who will give you the kiss that curls your toes. He just hasn't come along yet. You cannot settle for anything or anyone less. I feel incredibly lucky that Cameron can give me that. What about George? Does his kiss curl your toes?"

Brandi picked up her coffee cup and leaned back in her chair. "We haven't kissed yet. Since I don't know the first thing about courting, I'm letting him set the pace.

When he's ready, he'll kiss me." She sipped her coffee. "I think you and Cameron were made for each other. I can't tell you how I know or why I feel that way, because you just met, but I do. If you both give it a chance, I think you'll have a good marriage. My parents had a good marriage until Mama died. Papa didn't really know what to do with me then, but he did the best he could. He taught me about farming and Mama taught me to cook. When Papa died, I tried to get a job as a cook. No one would even consider me because I was too young."

Her voice changed, and she started to talk like she was someone high and mighty. In other words—a pompous ass.

Brandi bent an arm at the elbow and then bent her wrist, so her palm was facing down. "You can't possibly know enough to cook for our customers. Ha!" She shoved her arms into the air. "I could cook food ten times better than any of those fancy chefs they had." Her shoulders slumped, "So I took the only job I seemed to be qualified for."

Eve put her hand across the kitchen table and grasped Brandi's hand. "You did what you had to. Don't beat yourself up about it. That was then, this is now, and you are Brandi Johnson, cook extraordinaire. You really are good. I haven't eaten this well in ages. But enough of this. What will we do today?"

"Clean the house."

"Sounds good. With both of us doing it, we'll get

done before lunch and then we can go do some shopping."

"I can't. I have an outing with George this afternoon. Besides what would we shop for. We have food enough for a few more days."

"We can always find something to buy."

"Well, if we go to the mercantile first we could get some yarn, so we can knit new socks to wear with our boots. After the mercantile we can come back and clean the house and then I'll have my bath."

Eve looked away with a stab of regret or was it guilt? She should have learned more of what her mother wanted her to. "I don't know how to knit. Mama never got around to teaching me much of the girl stuff. Papa was too busy teaching me how to play cards."

"Well then I think it's high time you learned. I'd also like to take a bath before my outing with George Clarendon this afternoon."

"Perhaps you could invite him to join us for supper sometime. I know we're having the bachelor deputies tonight."

Brandi grimaced and slowly shook her head. "I don't know, isn't that kind of forward for a woman to make that suggestion? We've only gone out a couple of times."

Eve put both her hands around the still warm cup, easing the cold she felt. "I don't know, but we're in the untamed West now. I figure we can make our own rules and I say invite him to supper…well only if you like him."

"I'll think about it and if the outing goes well, I might just do that. If we're going shopping early, we should get going."

"Right." Eve stood. "It's a little chilly and I think I'll put on a sweater."

"Me, too. Meet you in the front room." Brandi headed to her bedroom.

Eve finished the last bit of her coffee and put her cup in the sink. Then she went to get her sweater.

I hope everything goes well for Brandi today. I'd really like her to find some happiness after the life she's had foisted on her.

CHAPTER ELEVEN

The day was lovely for early May. Eve could hardly believe she'd been there for nearly two weeks or that she'd been sleeping next to Cameron for that amount of time without making love.

He'd been very gentle with her, not pushing her to make love, but now she was ready. The green trees and flowers that were just starting to come up reminded her that if she wanted children, she had to make love. Besides, she and Cameron had been holding each other every night and now she was ready to take their relationship to where it should be…intimate.

The first flowers she saw were purple and white with little yellow stamen. She'd gone outside to take in the warm summery-like day and noticed the flowers. Eve picked one and took it back inside. She found Cameron in the living room just before he left for work.

"Cameron, what is this flower?"

"It's a Columbine. They're usually one of the first flowers to bloom."

"I think they're pretty. I might pick some for the table when we have more of them. For now, I think I'll bake some bread, today. Fresh bread, hot from the oven, is always so good." She closed her eyes and made yummy sounds.

"Can you have it just coming out of the oven when I get home for lunch?"

"No, but it will be fresh when Sam and Jake come over for dinner tonight."

"That'll have to do." He gave her a deep kiss, then ran his fingers around her jaw. "See you at lunch."

Eve was finally starting to get used to his kisses. At least she didn't stop everything, mesmerized by them, anymore. She could function now.

Brandi stopped on her way to her bedroom with sheets that had been on the line overnight. "Oh, I'd like to learn. I'll watch you."

"All right. We picked up everything we need at the mercantile the other day. Basically, it's flour, sugar, yeast, salt, a little lard or butter and water. Meet me in the kitchen."

Eve gathered all the ingredients while waiting for Brandi.

She walked in. "Okay, I'm ready to learn how to make bread. I've never tried it because I found it daunting to even think about."

"It's easy. Watch." Eve mixed up the dough, kneaded it for seven or eight minutes, put it in a clean bowl, covered it with a dishtowel and left it to rise.

"That's it until it rises just higher than the top of the bowl. That takes several hours. Then I'll punch it down, knead it again, separate it in half and put the dough in the bread pans and let it rise again. When it is about an inch above the top of the pans, I'll put the bread in the oven and bake it for about fifty-five minutes."

---

*E*ve baked the bread in time for supper with Sam Chism and Jake LeRoy who brought his daughter Jodie.

Cameron and Eve sat at the ends of the table, Jake and his daughter, Jodie on one side and Sam and Brandi on the other.

Brandi had outdone herself with the roast beef. The rosemary and thyme butter made the roast very tasty and the gravy was fantastic, unlike anything Eve had tried before.

Eve's fresh bread only added to the meal.

Jake's daughter, Jodie, was twelve and very grown up for her age.

"Tell me, Jodie, do you take care of your dad by yourself or do you have help from an aunt or someone?" asked Eve.

The pretty girl, with porcelain skin and nearly black hair, grinned. "Daddy and I take care of each other, don't we, Daddy?"

Jake smiled indulgently at his daughter, who was his spitting image. "We do." Jake looked at Eve. "Her mother passed when Jodie was just five. It's been just her and me since."

"I'm sorry for your loss," said Eve.

"Thank you," said Jake.

The silence while everyone ate was easy and natural.

"What about you, Sam? Ever been married?" asked Brandi.

"Nope," he grinned. "You offering?"

Brandi laughed. "Not tonight, check with me next week."

Sam set his knife and fork down and clasped his hands over his heart. "You wound me, madam."

Cameron laughed. "I forgot to tell you ladies that Sam is something of a character around the office."

"I'd marry Miss Brandi any day." Sam protested.

Brandi shook her head and then laughed again.

When supper came to an end and the guests left, Eve sent Brandi and Cameron both into the living room while she did the dishes. She thought that was only fair since Brandi had prepared such a fantastic supper.

After she finished, she stopped by the living room. "I'm headed to bed now. Thank you for a great meal, Brandi. I'll see you in the morning."

"Is that a promise or a threat?" laughed Brandi.

Eve chuckled. "I didn't know you had such a good sense of humor. And it's a promise. I'll never threaten you." She walked on to the bedroom and undressed. Eve didn't put on her nightgown but got into bed and quickly covered up. The room had taken on a chill since the sun went down.

Cameron entered. "I had to lock the doors."

He stripped and got into bed then leaned up on his elbow facing her.

"I'm cold." She scooted toward him.

"I'm hot, together we'll be just right." He lay back and put his arm out so she could cuddle with him.

Eve turned onto her side and laid her arm over his chest. "You are warm. I like it."

"I like feeling you next to me." He squeezed her to him.

She lifted herself and looked at him before she took his lips in a kiss, their lips melding together.

Eve kissed his chin, then his neck and down to his

chest. "I've been here and we've been sleeping together for almost two weeks. I'd like us to make love. I'd like to make a baby if we can. I still can't guarantee that we can, but I'd like to try. I want a child, Cameron. A baby who looks just like you." Whatever happened, this was right. She'd never felt more strongly that making love was the right thing for them to do. Now. Tonight.

"And I'd like a little girl who looks just like her mama." He scooted closer and then reached under the covers and pulled her to him. Cameron kissed her deeply.

She wrapped her arms about him and relaxed against the pillows all the while kissing him back.

"Are you sure, Eve? I want very much to make love to you."

"Then why are you talking?"

Cameron laughed and then proceeded to make sweet love to her.

Would she feel as strongly in the morning that she'd been in the right?

⁂

The next morning, Eve was in an exceptionally good mood. She and Cameron had held each other most of the night. She'd never snuggled with Johnny, and now she knew for certain that Johnny was a terrible lover. She hadn't known what she was missing. Now that she did, she wouldn't ever have to give up making love. Cameron seemed to enjoy it as much as she did. She dressed, while he watched her and then went to the kitchen, leaving him in bed.

Not even five minutes later, he entered the kitchen, whistling.

"You seem awfully happy this morning." She grinned.

"I am, wife." He took her in his arms and kissed her soundly.

"Wow, can I expect that every morning?"

Cameron took his chin in his fingers and looked up toward the ceiling. "That depends on what kind of night I had and last night I had a very good night."

Her voice low she whispered against his lips, "So did I." Then she kissed him again. "Now though I have to make coffee. Brandi will be up in a little bit." Just thinking about the things they did and the wonderful way she felt was almost like feeling it all again.

Cameron had been so attentive. She'd felt like she was the most important person in the world. Last night she would have bet on it.

"Brandi is already up." She entered the kitchen. "And you two might as well sit because you're just in my way."

"Well, I guess we'd better sit." She stepped out of Cameron's arms and grabbed three coffee cups before she sat.

Brandi prepared breakfast. She fried bacon and then in the grease she fried the eggs. She'd sliced bread and toasted it in another skillet, turning it once before she removed the slices from the pan and buttered them.

"This looks great, Brandi," said Eve.

"I agree. I've never eaten so well," added Cameron.

Silence reigned while they ate until Cameron tipped back in his chair and rubbed his stomach. "That was a fine breakfast, Brandi. Thank you."

"You're welcome."

"Yes," agreed Eve. "Now, I'll do the dishes." She gathered their plates and silverware and took them to the sink.

"And I'll let you." Brandi sipped her coffee.

Cameron stood and got his hat from the pegs by the back door. Then he went to the sink, turned Eve around and kissed her. "Goodbye, wife. I'll see you at lunch." He donned his hat and walked out the door.

"Will his kisses always leave you speechless?" Brandi chuckled.

Eve took a deep breath and slowly let it out. "Lord, I hope so." Then she smiled, went to the stove, retrieved the bucket of hot water and prepared to wash the dishes.

When she had the water ready, she turned toward Brandi, reading the newspaper at the table. "I need to get material at the mercantile, along with all the things I need to sew with. Do you want to come?"

"I don't know. Carl makes me nervous. I know he's interested in me and the fact I'm seeing George, doesn't seem to make a difference to him."

While she washed the dishes, she conversed with Brandi. "I understand, but he has got to give up sooner or later and let's hope sooner. Where did George take you last time?"

"He took me to the schoolhouse and showed me what he did. His home is next to the school. A little cabin with one bedroom. We didn't go inside but he told me about it."

"Well, that's safe enough, I guess. What else did you do?" *I really thought they'd go on a picnic or something along that line.*

"We went to a restaurant for dessert and coffee and talked…just talked. It was nice to talk to a man, to have someone interested in what I thought and what I believed. He's a good man but I don't know if I'm good enough for him."

Eve widened her eyes. "If you had a nice time, why in the world would you think you're not good enough?"

Brandi frowned. "Because he's much too good for the likes of me."

Eve dried her hands, walked over to the table and sat. "He is not. You are as good or better than any man in this town. Don't you believe otherwise. Now let's go to the mercantile. You can pick out some yarn for a baby blanket. I want two. One pink and one blue."

Brandi smiled. "Are you planning on having twins?"

"Maybe, you just never know."

"I know you finally made love last night. You and Cameron were just too happy this morning. It's different when you like the person you're with. At least it was for me…with Robert."

Eve grinned. "It's different when you're with someone who knows what they're doing. Johnny, my dead husband, didn't know his butt from a hole in the ground."

Brandi laughed. "I cannot believe you just said that."

Eve laughed. "I could have said worse. I spent a lot of time around men and they have the worst mouths."

"I know. Believe me I know." Brandi stood. "Let's get shawls or sweaters and go. I want to get back home. For some reason I feel safer being at home."

"I understand. I feel the same. I think part of it is

having a home. Not a room somewhere." *I can't believe I already think of this house as my home. It's been so long since I had a real home. I like the feeling.*

Brandi smiled. "That's it exactly. This is how I felt before Mama and Papa died."

Eve wondered how long she would feel like she was living someone else's life. Would she always feel like Brandi? That she wasn't good enough for Cameron, good enough for the life she had now?

CHAPTER TWELVE

*S*unday, May 10, 1863

"*C*ameron, come on," hollered Eve from the kitchen. "Brandi and I are ready to go to Earl and Blanche's for Sunday supper. We've got the rolls you said we'd bring."

Brandi stood next to the sink finishing her coffee. Then she put the empty cup in the sink.

"I'm here, no need to shout," said Cameron from behind her where she stood at the sink.

"Oh, my gosh," her hand flew to her mouth and stopped her scream. "You sneak up on me on purpose, I know you do."

Brandi chuckled.

Cameron grinned and then frowned. "Who me?" He laughed.

"Yes, you." She swatted his chest. "Let's go. I want to see how Earl is fairing. Since we've missed the last two Sundays, you haven't seen him for almost three weeks. I predict he's on the mend. Maybe all he needed was to have you settled, and now you have me. That makes you settled."

Brandi widened her eyes.

Eve was sure she was just as anxious as Brandi since she knew Earl's secret, too.

Questions would be asked today when Cameron saw Earl, if she was not mistaken.

When they arrived at the Ralstons', Cameron knocked on the door.

Blanche answered and was all smiles. "Hello, come in." She looked over at Eve. "Thank you for the rolls. Normally, I would make them, but I am having problems with my hands and can't knead dough like I used to. Biscuits are about all I can do now."

"I understand," said Eve. "We'll always bring the bread from now on. And I don't mind making extra bread each week and providing for you. You've always given Cameron and now Brandi and me Sunday suppers, it's time we helped out."

"Sure." Cameron frowned. "If I'd known, I'd have stopped by the bakery on Saturday and gotten the bread and rolls."

Blanche walked to Cameron and wrapped her arms around him. "I couldn't ask you. I'd always made everything for our meals together, and I didn't want to change that."

He hugged her back, leaning and resting his head on top of hers. "You're too easy on me. But I love you for it."

The older woman patted his chest.

"Where's Earl?" asked Cameron. "Does he need my help?"

"Oh, no, dear. He's been improving every day. He can walk on his own, and his color has returned. It's a miracle."

Eve almost laughed. Instead she placed a hand over her mouth and cleared her throat. "Well, that's wonderful."

"What's wonderful?" Earl boomed as he entered the living room.

"Earl?" Cameron's eyes were wide.

"Yes, my boy. I'm almost good as new. Still get tired and need to take a nap in the afternoon, but other than that, I feel fully recovered."

Cameron ran his hand behind his neck. He turned around and then back again. "Bu…but you were on your death bed."

"So I was. So I was." He patted his chest. "I don't know what happened. I've just been getting better by the day. Let's go to the kitchen, shall we?"

"Yes, let's," said Blanche. "I've got dinner ready and waiting. The table is set. All we need to do is sit."

Eve and Brandi followed Earl and Cameron, who followed Blanche.

Eve looked over at Brandi, who wore the same grin that Eve herself probably wore. She was surprised by the amount of recovery Earl had been willing to admit to. Completely recovered! She could hardly keep herself from laughing.

When they arrived in the kitchen, Earl and Cameron sat in the same chairs they had when Cameron and Eve had married.

Eve followed Blanche to the stove. "Can I help serve?"

"Why yes, dear, that would be extremely helpful. I've got the chicken, potatoes, and gravy in the warming oven. Brandi, dear, would you grab the butter crock from the counter please?"

"Of course," answered Brandi.

Eve pulled the dishes from the warming oven and handed them to Blanche who set them on the table. She had serving spoons already on the table and inserted them in the appropriate dishes.

"Earl, would you carve the chicken, please? It's a nice roaster, almost as big as a small turkey."

The chicken was the largest Eve had ever seen. When she was little, her father would kill a chicken periodically and they'd have it for Sunday dinner, but the birds were never this big. That was before her father had taken up poker to make a living at, before her mother had died. Then they were just another farm family, trying to eek a living out of the dirt. This memory didn't make her smile, just the opposite, tears filled her eyes instead. She dabbed at her eyes with her hanky.

"Eve? Are you all right?" Cameron put his arm around her shoulders.

"Yes, I was just remembering what life was like when I was a little girl. I'm fine really. Let's sit." Eve watched Earl. He had a big smile on his face and no trace of powder anywhere. He was healthy as an ox.

"I'm so glad you're feeling so well," said Cameron, who sat on Earl's right, next to Eve. "We were all genuinely concerned. I thought sure I'd be burying you soon."

Earl stopped carving, put down the knife and fork and patted Cameron's arm. "I'm sorry to have made you worry so much. I don't know what I had. Some sort of flu maybe. Who knows? But I'm better now and intend to enjoy myself, especially now that you're married. How is married life treating you two?"

"Very well." Cameron covered Eve's hand on the table. "We've had some lengthy discussions about what we each expect out of this marriage. About the only thing we completely agree on is that we both want children."

"Well, that's a good thing to agree on," Blanche smiled at Eve. "Earl and I can't wait for you to have a baby we can spoil. Isn't that right dear?"

"Brandi has said much the same thing, haven't you?" asked Eve.

"Yes, I'd love to have a baby around. I hope to have children someday, too," said Brandi. "But until I do, I can spoil yours."

Blanche clapped her hands. "Oh, wouldn't it be wonderful if you both had babies?"

"I need to get married first." Brandi waved her hands in front of her. "And I don't know if that will ever happen."

Eve narrowed her eyes at Brandi. "Of course, it will happen. You just haven't met the right man."

"There are all kinds of men who want to marry me, but that's because I'm one of the few women in town not married."

"What about George?" Eve removed her hand from under Cameron's and placed it in her lap. "He seemed a genuinely nice man and he liked you a lot. He talked only to you the entire way from Denver. I don't think anyone else in the coach existed for him. And you've gone on several outings with him."

Brandi blushed to the top of her forehead. "He's nice enough I suppose. I haven't seen him since we went on that last outing, so I guess he wasn't that interested, after all."

Eve reached across the table and took Brandi's hand in hers. "Give him time. He did say he buys books for the children. Perhaps he has to take the books to them, and who knows how long that process will take."

"I suppose that's true. I guess I can wait a little longer and be a bit more patient."

"That's my girl." Eve glanced at Cameron. He was staring at Earl. She was afraid the jig was up.

"Earl, I'd like to ask you a question, and I'd like an honest answer." Cameron rested his elbows on the table and steepled his fingers.

"Certainly, my boy, what can I help you with?" Earl continued to carve the chicken.

"Did you just start getting better this week? Or did it start when Eve and I got married?"

Earl swallowed hard and his hands shook a bit. He paused his carving. "I'm not sure when, exactly. Why do you ask?"

Cameron tilted his head and pursed his lips. "I just thought it was quite the coincidence that you are better now that I'm married."

"Yes, well, Cam, about that, I—"

"If I'd known not being married was making you sick, I might have gotten hitched sooner…but I really don't think so." He looked at Eve. "I never found anyone I wanted to marry."

"Cameron," said Blanche. "Do you really think

now is the time for this conversation?" She nodded her head toward Eve.

Eve placed her elbows on the table and rested her chin on the heel of a hand. "No, I think now is as good a time as any for this discussion. Don't mind me."

Brandi, eyes wide, sat back in her chair.

Blanche, a frown on her face, let out a long breath and slumped in her chair.

Cameron gazed at everyone at the table and then back to Earl. "What is going on here? I get the feeling everyone here is in on the joke but me."

The judge set the carving utensils by the platter with the chicken and collapsed in his chair. "There is no one to blame but me. I set this up with Doc, because I couldn't have achieved it without him to make it believable."

"Believable?" Cameron's color was rising, and his voice was getting softer and deeper. "What needed to be believable?"

"I needed for you to believe that I was sick and getting progressively sicker. That was the only way I could make sure you were married, and I wanted you to have a family. Blanche and I aren't going to be around forever. You needed your own family…a wife and kids."

"Family?" Cameron's jaw clenched and he

breathed faster. His veins pumped as his pulse speeded up.

Eve was afraid Cameron would have a heart attack before the judge ever got the whole thing out. "Oh, good grief. Would you just tell him?" She jumped up and looked over at Cameron. "He's not sick. Has never been sick. He wanted to see you married, so he put on this farce and then, when that didn't seem to be working, he put the ad in the papers. I noticed he was wearing makeup the first day I came. I found out why when you helped him to bed. You were too close to the situation to see what he was doing or perhaps you didn't want to believe you friend would trick you."

"So, you knew, too? Before or after we married?"

"Does it matter?"

"It matters."

She knew he was angry, but so was she. *Why did I marry him? Because I was more attracted to him than I'd been any man in a long time, that's why.* "Fine. Before."

He sat up straight, like a rod was in his back. "Why did you marry me, if you knew he was faking?"

She breathed out...loudly. "I'm beginning to wonder myself."

"So why did you?"

She paced the kitchen. "You know why. Because I was attracted to you and since I came to get a husband, I figured you were the best of the lot." She watched his face go from bewilderment to anger and then to...amusement? What? "Do you find this situation funny?"

He grinned. "As a matter of fact I do. Neither of us wanted this marriage, and now we're stuck."

"So we are, in more ways than one." She turned, calmly walked out of the kitchen to the living room and slammed the door on her way out.

"*W*ell, heck." Cameron stood and ran after her.

Brandi looked after them. "Well, shall we continue with supper? They'll be back after they're done getting mad and making up, or they might just go home to make up, in either case, I'm staying here." She served herself a spoon of mashed potatoes and picked the bowl up and passed it. "Here you go, Blanche."

*E*ve heard the pounding of boots hitting the dirt behind her. She looked behind her, saw him, lifted her skirts, and began to run.

"Eve! Stop!"

"Leave me alone!"

Suddenly, her skirts slipped from her hand, and she fell, landing on her side. "Oww." She sat up and tried to stand but fell to the ground again. "Gosh darn it."

He skidded to a halt beside her and dropped to one knee. "Eve, honey. I'm sorry. Here, let me help you." He stood and lifted her to her feet.

As soon as he released her, she hollered and collapsed.

"Whoa, there." He caught her and swung her up into his arms. "I'm taking you to Doc's. Hopefully, you haven't broken anything."

She lay in his arms, crying and refusing to put her arms around his neck.

"Eve."

"Don't talk to me." She sniffled and took the hanky from her sleeve. Dabbing at her eyes, she sniffled again. "We should divorce. You don't want to be married to me and, even though I chose you, you didn't have a choice with me."

"I choose you."

"You can find someone—you choose me?" She looked up at him, eyes wide. Her pulse raced and she needed to hear him say it again. Johnny'd never said nice things to her. In the two years they were married he didn't say he loved her even once.

"Yes, I choose you. We can continue to get to

know each other, because Lord knows I don't want to go through this process again."

"Living with you hasn't been easy for me either, you know. I'm used to being alone. Sharing space isn't something I've done for five years or more, actually, since Johnny was gone more often than he was home."

He lifted an eyebrow. "So, I've never shared with anyone and I think we were doing rather well. Give us another chance. We've only been together for three weeks. And who knows? You could already be expecting."

"We won't know that for a couple of months. Are you sure you want to keep me around that long?"

"Yes, I want to keep you around. I want to give this marriage a try, and we need more than three weeks to know if it works or not."

He walked up the path to the doctor's office. "Now, dry your eyes and let's see if you will be okay."

"I think I just sprained it. I'm really bad with pain."

"I would say, if you're expecting that you better get used to it. Friends have told me their wives said it's the most pain they've ever known, but that they would go through it again to have their baby."

"You're not helping here. Don't like pain...remember?"

He bent and opened the door without setting her down. Then he walked inside and closed the door with his boot.

"Doc?"

"What do you want, Cameron?" Doc Whitaker said as he walked out of the hallway, his white hair standing up and out from his head like tufts of cotton. "What's the matter with this woman?"

"She tripped—"

She crossed her arms over her chest. "I was chased."

"Fine, I chased her and she tripped. She might have a sprained ankle, but that is for you to determine."

"That's right. I am the doctor, after all. Follow me."

The doctor led the way to the back room which he also called the surgery.

"Set her down on the table and I'll take a look at her ankle. I'm Doctor Whitaker, by the way."

"Eve Neal."

Cameron carefully set her down trying not to hurt her. He noticed she closed her eyes and grimaced when he set her on the table.

"I'm sorry," he whispered.

She nodded. "It's okay, I know you didn't mean to hurt me."

"Remember that when he starts messing with your leg."

Eve smiled. "I'll try."

"Out of my way, Cameron." Doc set the towel he'd used to dry his hands on the table. "Now, young lady, let's see what we have going on here." He removed her boot and felt her swollen ankle.

Eve cried as he moved the joint around.

"Well, the good thing is, nothing appears to be broken. The bad news is that you definitely sprained it. You'll have to keep it elevated for a few days and keep ice on it for at least the first day. I'll wrap it tight so you don't move it." He looked over at Cameron. "Bring her back in two weeks, and we'll see how it's doing then. I expect she'll be walking on it again by that time."

"What about the pain?" asked Cameron.

"Yes, I'm not good with pain," said Eve.

"You can take half a teaspoon of laudanum every four hours." He walked over to the cabinet above the counter holding his wash basin. "I'll give you one dose here. I want you to take a second dose when you get home. Then every four hours after that for just three days."

"Okay, I'll make sure she takes it."

"I don't think that will be a problem," said Eve. "Bad with pain, remember?"

Doc gave her the laudanum in half a glass of

water. "Drink it all down even though it tastes nasty. It will help but you'll still have pain when I wrap it."

She drank it and then closed one eye and clenched her jaw at the taste. Eve then braced herself with her hands behind her while she sat up.

Cameron took the glass back to the counter and returned with a round ball of heavy gauze. "I'd prefer you lie down, please." Doc put the cloth beside her.

She lay back on the table.

He wrapped her ankle around and around, tight but not enough to stop the blood circulation to her foot.

"What do I owe you, Doc?" asked Cameron.

"Three dollars and fifty cents ought to do it."

Cameron reached into his pocket and gave Doc a five-dollar gold piece. "Put the rest on our account. We'll need it when she is expecting, anyway."

"All right," said Doc. "Cameron, come back and get her crutches. She'll need those for a few days, at least."

"Will do."

Doc looked at Eve. "I'll see you in two weeks."

"Thanks, Doc. It does feel better since you wrapped it."

He smiled. "Good." Doc looked over at Cameron. "Take her home and give her that laudanum. I want her to sleep, if possible."

"Goodbye, Doc," said Eve.

"Yes, goodbye Doc. I'll give her the medicine and keep watch to see that she sleeps."

Cameron picked her up and carried her home. He helped her out of her clothes and into a nightgown. "I hate this thing," he held up the offending garment. "But you'll be more comfortable with it on, since you'll be in bed and want to sit up occasionally."

She sniffled. Her leg hurt, she was mad at Cameron and she couldn't even stand and bake. What else could go wrong?

CHAPTER THIRTEEN

*M*ay 22, 1863

*E*ve was seeing the doctor today. She knew her ankle was healed because she was walking without pain. As a matter of fact, she was walking to the doctor's office. If that didn't convince him she was well, nothing would.

She walked into the office. The doctor was leaning against the desk in the outer office with his arms crossed over his chest.

"Well, you finally got here. I figured you would be the first one in. Ready to get the okay and get back in your shoes?"

She held out her foot. "Already am, Doc. I just came in to show you I'm healed."

"So it would appear. I still want to check you over though. Come on back."

She followed him back to the same room she was in before...the surgery. Eve hopped up on the table and sat with her legs dangling over the side.

Doc Whitaker raised her leg and moved the ankle around in a circle and forward and back. Then he lowered her leg. "Well, you're right. You are completely healed. Now I don't want to see you back here until you're expecting.

"You won't Doc. I'll do my best to not be accident prone."

"See that you do."

*B*uck Stone and his brothers rode three abreast as they entered Silver City. They'd ridden hard to get here as soon as they had, but his wound had opened along the way and he needed to see a doctor.

The three of them stopped by the Silver Nugget saloon. Each of them downed a shot of whiskey.

Buck waved over the paunchy, balding barkeep. "Another for each of us. You got a doctor in this town?"

"Sure do. One block west of here next to the Silver City Hotel."

"Thanks." Buck threw three dollars on the counter. Whiskey was expensive in this town. They'd have to camp outside of town if they were to have any money to eat and drink. "How many saloons you got here, anyway?"

The barkeep chuckled. "More than thirty, now. Seems like a new one opens every day and ain't none of 'em lacking customers."

"Crap," he said to his brothers. "It's gonna take us a long time to find her unless we get real lucky."

"We ain't never been lucky at all," said Billy, Buck's youngest brother. He was blonde and blue eyed, took after their ma.

"That's the truth," said Jack, the middle brother. He looked just like Buck, brown hair and brown eyes, like their Mexican bandit pa.

***

*T*he next day, Brandi walked in from another outing with George and was all smiles. "You were right, Eve. He was delivering the books to the students. They don't always come to school, that's why he has to get books every year. He says he—"

"Hold on." Eve put her hands in front of her. "Stop. Slow down. You're talking a mile a minute."

She laughed. "Sorry. I'm happy. I really like George and the thought that he didn't like me nearly broke my heart."

"I know it did, but I'm glad you got it worked out."

"I do and he's coming to supper on Friday if you and Cameron don't mind."

"Of course, we don't mind. Cameron already said anytime you want to invite George is fine."

"Okay, I'm just making sure."

Her eyes widened, "What if George doesn't like how I cook? What if—"

"Stop looking for reasons not to invite him."

"What if he doesn't want to come?"

"You'll cross that bridge when you come to it." *He better come or I'm having a word with young Mr. Clarendon.*

July 6, 1863

. . .

*E*ve left Doc Whitaker's office with a giant smile on her face. She had some great news for Cameron and tried to think just how to tell him. She'd tell him first and Brandi second, though that would be tough since she'd see Brandi when she arrived at the house and she'd want to know what happened at the doctor's. So, instead of going home she went to the marshal's office to find Cameron.

Reaching the office, she knocked once and then entered. Robert Lee was at the desk. In front of the desk was a wooden slat-backed chair, but Eve was too nervous to sit.

"Hi Robert. Is Cameron around?"

"Sure, he's in the back." He pointed at the chair. "Have a seat. I'll get him for you. He's just checking on a couple of prisoners who came in last night. Be right back."

"I'm fine standing, but thanks."

"Sure. Oh, by the way, I'm a father. Methabel gave me a son two nights ago."

Eve smiled. "Well congratulations. That's wonderful news."

"I think so." He grinned and puffed out his chest a little. "I'll get Cameron for you now."

"Thank you."

Cameron walked into the office a few minutes later. "Well, hi there. To what do I owe this surprise?"

"I have some news and I wanted to share it with you first. Do you have a place we can talk?"

He put an arm around her waist and moved them away from the doorway to the back. "Right here is fine. Robert will be with the new prisoners for a while. Now, what do you have to tell me?"

Cameron held her by the elbow with his eyes narrowed.

She saw by his demeanor that he was anxious about what she had to say. "I won't keep you in suspense. I went to the doctor today. I haven't been feeling well most mornings. If I eat, I throw it up. Anyway, I wanted to know what was wrong."

His eyebrows furrowed with worry. "Why didn't you tell me you weren't feeling well? I'd have taken you much sooner."

She lifted a hand and cupped his face.

He leaned into her hand.

Eve's pulse raced and butterflies fluttered around her stomach. "I didn't want to worry you and turns out it wouldn't have helped, anyway. Cameron, I'm expecting. We're having a baby."

His eyes widened. "A baby? Really?"

"Yes, really." She grinned and wrapped her arms around his neck. "Looks like the first time was a charm, but that doesn't mean we can't continue to practice, just because I'm more fertile than I thought.

I guess it was Johnny who couldn't father a child. It wasn't me, at all."

He didn't respond except to give her the biggest kiss.

She hung on and rode the wave of feelings. Love. Joy. Happiness.

When they finally broke apart, both were breathless.

I want so much to tell you I love you, but I'm afraid you won't feel the same way, and I couldn't stand that especially now. I'd rather not know.

"I'll see you at home tonight. We'll celebrate."

"I'll bake a pie for dessert. I haven't told Brandi, yet. With her and George getting along so well, we might have a wedding here soon, and then a baby. Baby for us. Wedding for them. Sorry, I'm rambling."

Cameron shook his head and smiled. "I think that's okay. You're excited, so am I. And now that Earl is well, he and Blanche will be over the moon."

"That they will. And I'll tell them, if they ever pull another stunt like the one that got me here, I won't let them see the baby. I think that will have more weight than saying I'll kill them. I'm going home to tell Brandi. See you at supper." She kissed him lightly on the lips and started to step away.

"Oh no, you don't." He pulled her back to him. Then he took her face between his palms and kissed her like he had the day they got married. When he pulled back, he gazed at her. "Thank you for giving me a child. You can't imagine how happy I am."

"Yes, I can, because that's how happy I am, too." She walked out the door and headed home. *I'd hoped he might tell me he loves me with this news, but he's only happy about the baby. I won't let that affect how I feel. She placed her hand on her stomach. I love this little one more than anything and his father does, too. That's what I have to concentrate on.*

***

$\mathcal{B}$uck Stone and his brothers were closing in on the lady gambler who'd gotten him shot and who cheated him out of his money. She was a dead woman. All he had to do was find her. They'd checked too many of the saloons for him to count. He didn't get that far in school before he'd quit going and joined his father in the family business—robbery, murder, and general mayhem. Then he'd brought his brothers in.

Now the three of them were on their way to another saloon in Silver City. Their money was running low, but he didn't get any information if he didn't buy a drink. So now he's the only one who had a shot when they went into a saloon.

The first barkeep told them there were more than thirty saloons inside the town limits. That blonde girlie couldn't evade them forever. She and that whore would be found and then he'd see about getting his revenge.

---

*E*ve was so happy. There was nothing that could take the smile off her face. At least she didn't think so…until she saw Buck Stone and his brothers. She'd just stepped into the shadows of the mercantile and didn't think they saw her, but she turned her back to them, nonetheless.

When she was sure they were gone, she picked up her skirts and ran back to the marshal's office. She opened the door and shut it quickly behind her. "Cameron," she cried.

He stood up from the desk as soon as she came in. "Eve. What's the matter?"

"They're here. The Stone brothers are here."

"Calm down. I have to arrest them. They're wanted for murder in Texas and the Colorado Territory. I have no choice."

"You can't. They'll see you as soon as you walk in and kill you before you can do anything. I can help."

"No. I know what you want and I won't use you as bait."

"But they're looking for me."

"No. That's the end of it. I don't want to hear any more about it. I'm not letting you risk your life and that of our child. My deputies and I are quite capable of doing our jobs."

"But—"

"Eve, I'm walking you home and then my deputies and I are going to look for Stone and his brothers."

"You don't know what they look like."

He grinned. "I do, you told me, remember."

She worried he would never know them. Too many men could fit the description she gave him. "It would be easier for me to show you. There are many, many saloons for them to check thinking they'll find me. And many men who look and dress like they do. Let me go to the Red Lily and play for a few nights. They are sure to find me. They only know me as the *girlie in the red dress*."

"The dress you keep in the back of the closet?"

She widened her eyes. "You've seen it. I thought it was pretty much out of sight."

He cocked his head and frowned. "I'm the marshal. I need to know what my wife is hiding. Besides that closet is too small, as you told me the day you arrived, to hide anything much less a red dress."

She looked down and said softly, "I'd have told you if you asked me."

"I didn't need to. Once I saw the dress, I knew what you wore it for. Just didn't know why you kept it."

She put her hands on her hips. "In case I needed it. I didn't know if this marriage," she pointed back and forth between them, "would work or not. I needed to have a backup, so I kept the dress in case I ever had to go back to gambling. And I still might."

He narrowed his eyes and dropped his chin. "Not with my child you won't."

Suddenly, he looked extremely dangerous, but she knew he wouldn't hurt her. "Don't threaten me, Cameron. I don't like it and I don't react well."

"Eve, I will always come after you. Always."

She didn't know how to take that and studied his face for clues to his meaning. Was he coming after her because she carried his child or because he loved her?

---

*C*ameron walked Eve back home, his hand on his gun. He didn't put an arm around her, and she missed it. But they were fighting, so she supposed that was the reason. Or maybe, said her more-rational self, he was keeping his arms free, so he could protect her, in case they ran into Buck and his brothers.

Now, she felt like an idiot. Life would be so much easier if she knew how Cameron felt about her.

If it wasn't July, she would have sworn the air became cold. She felt chilled to the bone and couldn't stop herself from shaking.

"Eve?"

"Yes."

"Are you all right? You're shaking like a leaf."

"I'm fine. No, I'm not fine. I don't want you to go after Stone. You don't know him, but he'll know you. He'll know you're the marshal, before he ever sees your badge. He'll kill you and who's going to stop him? Do you honestly think any of the men in the saloon will stop him after you're dead or, for that matter, before he shoots you?"

He put his left arm around her shoulders. "You don't give the men in this town enough credit. They know me and know I treat'em fair. They won't let Stone get away if he shoots me, plus I won't be going in alone. I'll have Robert with me and Sam and Jake. They sure won't let Stone get away. And with four of us there, he probably won't even make a move."

She crossed her arms over her chest. "It would be faster, easier and safer my way."

"It wouldn't be easier or safer for me if you're out there. I'd have heart palpitations every minute you're there. Don't you see?" He pushed a wayward strand of hair behind her ear. "I can't let you do something so dangerous, especially now. I won't take a chance on losing you."

The way he looked at her, she could almost believe he meant her and not just because of the baby, but she knew better.

She wasn't trying to be brave, but thought her idea was the best one and would work the fastest. Who knew who else might be wanted and trying to hide in Silver City? Who might see this situation as good a time as any to get rid of the marshal?

"Honey, why're you crying?"

She had a lump in her throat so big she didn't think she'd be able to talk. "Because I don't want you to die."

He stopped, took her in his arms and held her, letting her cry.

She noticed he also kept her back to the street so he could see the street but her face was hidden.

"Are you better now?"

She sniffled, took a hanky from her sleeve, and blew her nose. "Yes, I am actually."

"Look, when we get home, we'll talk. I need you to understand about my job and what I can and cannot do. Okay?"

Eve nodded.

"Let's get home then."

They weren't far from home when he'd stopped… only a couple of blocks.

Eve realized he could have just let her cry for those two blocks, Johnny would have, but Cameron stopped and held her. He cared. Maybe it wasn't just the baby he cared about. He'd let her cry more than once during the past three and a half months and neither of them knew about the baby then, so it had to be her he cared for. Right?

Finally reaching home Eve unlocked the door and entered the kitchen followed by Cameron.

Brandi looked up from the sink with a smile that quickly faded. "What's the matter?"

Eve went to Brandi and took her hands in hers. "Buck Stone is here with his brothers."

Brandi began to shake. "That's not possible. How? How would they find us?" She covered her face and began to cry. "Just when things were looking up...when things were looking good for once, they have to show up. Why can't they just die and make the world a better place?"

Eve wrapped her arms around Brandi. "Shh. Everything will be all right. Cameron will take care of it." She turned and speared her husband with her gaze. "Won't you, *dear*?"

"Yes. It's my job and I will arrest him or see him dead...his choice."

Eve looked up at him. "Let's hope his choice doesn't see you dead, too."

CHAPTER FOURTEEN

*E*ve pulled back so she could see Brandi's face. "Look, all the news today wasn't bad. I went to the doctor this morning, and I'm having a baby. Probably sometime in January. So those blankets you've been knitting will come in handy. I'm going to the mercantile tomorrow—"

Cameron moved next to them and shook his head. "Not tomorrow. Not until we have him behind bars."

Eve sucked in a deep breath and expelled it slowly before nodding. "You're right. We're liable to end up with a lot of baked goods if I can't sew. I need something to do. I'm not used to being idle."

He wrapped his arms around both of the women. "I don't mind having a lot of baked goods. If I have to, I'll take them down to my office. The men don't all have wives and will be exceedingly grateful for the treats."

"You should have told me that sooner, I'd have been baking double batches."

"I didn't want to wear you out."

She lifted a brow. "Oh, really?"

Brandi quit crying and seemed to be watching Eve and Cameron with interest.

Eve hoped she'd forget about the Stone Brothers for a little while.

Cameron ran a hand behind his neck. "Okay, I didn't think about it until now. I'm a bad boss."

Eve rolled her eyes. "You'll not get any sympathy from me." He had the audacity to grin.

"Can't blame a man for trying."

"Why don't you go back to work, while Brandi and I decide what we'll do this afternoon after the house is clean."

"Laundry?" he asked. "No, that's an outside job and I don't want you outside at all if you can help it."

"That's right," said Eve. "And there wouldn't be time in the afternoon for baking or sewing or knitting or anything else."

"Well, I'll leave you two ladies to it, and be sure and lock the doors. We've had a rash of break-ins lately. And Eve, wear your gun."

She looked at him, her eyebrows raised. "For the thief or the Stone brothers?"

"Both."

Cameron walked over and gave her a kiss.

Her eyes narrowed.

He sighed. "Just because we're having an argument, doesn't mean I'll stop kissing you goodbye." He looked at her, one eyebrow cocked. "And we won't take our argument into the bedroom. Agreed?"

She nodded. "Agreed."

He kissed her again, a quick peck on the lips and then walked out the door.

Eve locked the door behind him and then made sure the front door was locked. When she returned to the kitchen, Brandi was sitting at the table, staring into her coffee cup.

"What's on your mind? You're not shaking any more so I know it's not the Stone brothers being here, well at least that's not all of it."

Brandi sniffled and then blew her nose into a hanky. "I still haven't told George about my past."

Eve got the coffee pot and a cup. She filled her cup and refilled Brandi's before setting the pot back on the stove.

"Don't you think you should? I know it'll be difficult, and he might be angry at first, but he'll apologize later…you know he will."

"What if he doesn't? What if he just walks away?" A single tear rolled down her cheek.

"The man I've come to know wouldn't do that.

He's a good man and I believe he's in love with you. How about you? Are you in love with him?"

Brandi nodded, her voice was soft, hopeful. "I am. I finally feel like it's okay to believe good can happen after bad. That I deserve to have some happiness in this world. I don't know what I'll do when I lose him."

"First, don't talk like you've already lost him because you haven't and you won't. I believe he'll stand by you. Second, tell him. Don't speculate what he might say, find out. Knowledge is the only way you'll get some rest. I can tell you've not been sleeping well."

Brandi shrugged. "You don't do that with Cameron, why should I tell George. I didn't say anything about not sleeping because there's nothing you can do about it. So, what's the point?"

Eve reached over and took her hands in hers. "I'd have fixed you some tea and sat up with you. That's what friends are for. Do I have to come check on you like I would a child?"

Brandi laughed. "No, of course not."

"Then wake me up when you can't sleep. My goodness when the baby comes, we'll all probably be up at all hours. I need to talk to Methabel. I bet she can tell me all I need to know about birthing children. I know this was her first, but she must have a mama who told her what to do, don't you think?"

Brandi nodded. "She probably can."

"So, you'll tell George about your past and go from there, it's really the only thing you can do with the Stone brothers in town. You don't want to have him hear it on the street or from some *well-meaning* friend."

Her eyes widened "No, that would be awful."

Eve nodded. "Yes, it would. It would imply you don't trust him or love him enough to trust him."

"What about you? Does Cameron know all about you?"

"He knows I'm a gambler and was married once before. But I've never been with anyone since then."

Brandi's eyes widened. "Not even Daniel Calhoun?"

Remembering the handsome gambler, Eve smiled. "He wanted to, but I told him no. He was nice and he was handsome, but I also knew he only wanted some fun. He didn't want to settle down. I think I did… even then. Maybe that's why I jumped at being a mail-order bride and I got incredibly lucky. I could have been matched with one of those unwashed men we ran into our first day here."

"Yes, instead you got the most handsome man in town." Brandi grinned. "Next to George and Robert."

Eve chuckled. "Sam and Jake are no slouches in the handsome department."

Brandi nodded. "Yeah, that's true."

Eve shook her head and closed her eyes for a moment. "Look at us, talking about how handsome men are or aren't." Her lips twisted and her nostrils flared.

Brandi made a face that looked like she was about to vomit.

"The Stone brothers definitely aren't."

"Oh, heck no. I don't know how you did what you did. I couldn't have done it." Bile rose in her throat at just the thought of bedding those men. "I'd probably have been thrown out on the street the first time some ugly, old, hairy man came near me. I'd have screamed and run. I admire your fortitude."

She waved her hand away from her. "You wouldn't have starved or got assaulted. You knew something else to do. I decided if I was about to provide the entertainment for men anyway, I'd darn well get paid for it."

"That's why I admire you. You took your life by the horns." Eve raised her fists as though she was grabbing horns. "You didn't let some man decide what you were supposed to do."

"Is that the way you feel about Cameron? That he's deciding what you'll do and what you won't?"

"Right now? Yes. I have an idea that I'm sure would work but he says absolutely not."

"What's your idea?"

"I want to put on my red dress and go gamble. It

will get around town in nothing flat, and the Stone brothers will come to me."

Brandi shook her head. "I agree with Cameron. It's much too dangerous. You have a baby to think about now. You can't be putting yourself in danger like that. Buck Stone is liable to shoot before Cameron can stop him."

Eve's chest hurt, her heart hurt. Just the thought of losing Cameron, pulled at her gut. She put an elbow on the table and rested her chin in her hand. "I know but I also know it would work."

*B*randi knew she couldn't let Eve go gamble, but her plan really was a good one. She knew how to play, and she could wear the red dress, even if it would be tight on the bosom and a couple of inches too long. She could make it work. While Eve was in the kitchen contemplating how she would convince Cameron, Brandi would get the red dress and go in her stead.

She hurried to their bedroom, found the red dress, took it to her room and put it on. She still had the fifty dollars Eve gave her in her reticule. When she was ready, she slowly opened her bedroom door, peeked out and not seeing Eve, she hurried out the front door and headed to The Red Lily Saloon. It was the closest and she was less likely to see Cameron or one of his deputies on her way there. She'd gamble and the news of the lady gambler at the Red Lily would spread like wildfire through the town.

All she had to do was play until Cameron and Buck Stone arrived.

---

*E*ve had promised she wouldn't do it. She did have a new life to protect, and she couldn't risk herself like that. She'd tell Brandi what she decided, and Brandi would feel better about it, too.

She went looking for Brandi all over the house and couldn't find her. "Oh, my God." She ran to her bedroom and searched the closet for the red dress. It was gone. "Brandi what have you done?"

Eve ran out of the house, slamming the door shut behind her, and headed for The Red Lily Saloon.

---

*E*ve caught up with Brandi before she got anywhere near the Red Lily.

"Brandi, what in the world do you think you're doing? They'll know it's not me. Come with me." Eve took her by the arm and pulled her behind some bushes out of sight of the street. "Take off that dress."

"No." She shook her head. "You're right. This is the only way to get them."

"I agree, so give me the dress." Eve was already unbuttoning her dress as fast as she could.

Brandi slipped the dress over her head. "Eve, you don't have to do this. Cameron will be livid."

"Better me than you. I can keep them playing longer than you can. Long enough for the Stone brothers to hear about me and for Cameron to get there with his men."

Brandi slipped out of the dress and into the one Eve was wearing at the same time Eve donned her red dress. But this was life or death. Hers and Brandi's lives were at stake.

When they were both dressed again, Eve took Brandi by the shoulders. "Find Cameron. Tell him to get his men in place as soon as possible. This gossip will make it around town in nothing flat. Oh, and give me your reticule. That's got the money in it doesn't it?"

Brandi nodded and handed over the little bag. "Please take care. Sit with your back to the wall, if you can, just like you taught me."

Eve smiled. "I'll be as careful as I can. Now you go get Cameron. Hurry!"

The woman, who was like a sister to Eve, lifted her skirts and ran toward the sheriff's office.

Eve took a deep breath and rotated her neck. She

walked to the Red Lily and went in. "Lord, be with me."

---

*C*ameron saw Brandi running toward him.

He met her halfway. Cameron grabbed her by her upper arms and shook her. "Where is Eve?"

"I was going to go to the Red Lily instead of her and play so the Stones would find me. But she wouldn't let me. She caught me and we changed clothes. She sent me to find you and said for you and your deputies to get there because it won't take long for the Stones to hear about the blonde playing poker."

Cameron squeezed Brandi's shoulders, his stomach in knots. "Darn her. I forbade it."

"Oww, Cameron, you're hurting me."

He released her immediately. "I'm sorry. I'm out of my mind." He took off his hat and ran a hand through his hair.

"It's my fault. I'm sorry, Cameron. I only wanted those Stone brothers to get captured right away. It's too dangerous for Eve and me to have them running loose."

"I want you to go home. I don't need to worry about you, too."

"All right but let me know as soon as they're in custody. Do you have a spare weapon?"

"In the bottom left drawer of the bureau. You'll find the gun and spare ammunition, too. I'll send someone to tell you when they've been arrested. Now I must get my deputies so we can save my stubborn wifed. Go."

She turned and hurried toward the house.

He ran back to the office and hoped the rest of his men were there.

When he reached there, he slammed open the door. "I want all of you to come with me. I'll explain on the way."

Robert, Sam, and Jake snapped to attention.

Cameron checked his weapon.

His men did the same.

"Let's go." Cameron ran toward the Red Lily. This was one time he couldn't afford to be late.

CHAPTER FIFTEEN

The Red Lily was one of the better saloons in Silver City but was still not as nice as the ones in Ft. Worth. The men watched her as she came in. Followed her with their eyes but didn't stop her as she made her way to the poker tables.

Eve sat at the table with an open seat. The outside chair was the one open unfortunately, for her safety, but best for her scheme to work. The men behind her would have the best seats for her cleavage show until she started raking in the money. She'd already decided to give her winnings to George for the school kids.

"You sure you know how to play, little lady?" Asked one old miner.

"I can assure you she does."

The deep baritone was familiar. The voice belonged to Daniel Calhoun from Ft. Worth.

"Well, hi there, Handsome. I haven't seen you for several months. How's the world treating you?"

"Very good, Eve. How are you?"

"Never better, Daniel." She made sure to bend forward as she sat and let the men at the table get a peek at her cleavage. She hated this part, but there was no going back now. Eve had to give it her all or she needed to leave the table and take her chances. She thought the odds were better playing the game than leaving. "Whose deal is it?"

"Yours, dear Eve." Daniel handed her the deck.

Eve shuffled three times and then passed the deck to Daniel so he could cut it.

"Money plays?" She set the fifty dollars in the reticule on the table.

"Of course," said Daniel.

"Sure," said the other men, miners one and all.

"The game is draw, gentlemen. Ante up."

She dealt the hand. "Your bid, young man," she said to the old miner.

He laughed, showing two missing top teeth. "I think you need glasses, dearie. I ain't been young for forty years."

Eve grinned back at the man. "Could have fooled me, young man."

He cackled.

The bets were made and cards dealt. Eve ended up with a pair of kings.

The man to her left was the old miner. Next to him was probably the youngest at the table. He had dirty brown hair and a grimy mustache. The next man was fairly clean and wearing city clothes. He was obviously new to town by the looks of him. To her right was Daniel.

When it was her turn to bet, she folded. She wanted to make sure she didn't win the first few hands, and she also kept her cards close to her body so none of the bystanders could see her play.

After five hands, she allowed herself to really play. Now, if she lost the hand, it was because she really didn't have the cards.

From the corner of her eye, she saw Cameron enter with his deputies and spread out. Not too long after, the Stone brothers entered.

"Outta my way," hollered Buck Stone. He pushed his way up until he was right behind her.

With him behind her, Eve was extremely nervous but she had to trust that Cameron would arrest him before Buck shot her. She didn't let on she knew anything was happening behind her.

She heard Blondie and Red Bandana with Buck, too. Good, they were all together and Cameron could arrest them all at once.

"Buck Stone. You and your brothers are under

arrest for murder, bank robbery, and arson. Put your hands up or die right now," said Cameron.

Eve turned to look, her heart pounding so fast it felt like it would break out of her chest. She pulled her derringer from the special pocket in her skirt.

Buck had his gaze on her and pulled his gun. Shots rang out

Stone hit the floor.

Someone screamed.

Eve fell off her chair, a burning sensation in her side.

Cameron pushed chairs out of the way to reach her. "Eve. Eve. Honey, talk to me."

"Cam…shot…hurts…baby." She closed her eyes and the world went black.

---

*C*ameron, his heart pounding so hard he was sure everyone could hear it, picked Eve up in his arms and turned to take her to the doctor.

The group of men parted just like the Red Sea before Moses.

He ran through them, straight out the door, and didn't stop until he reached Doc Whitaker's.

Once at the doctor's office, he kicked the door with his boot. It wasn't latched well and opened. He hurried through.

"Doc! Doc!" he shouted and took a breath.

"I'm here." Doc ran up from the back of the offices, his unruly cotton white hair sticking out all over. "What's the matter with Eve?"

"She's been shot. Save her, please Doc."

"Bring her back to the surgery." The doctor turned and went back down the hall. "Lay her on the table. Where was she shot?"

"In the back."

"I see blood on the front of her body, so maybe the bullet went through. I'll need to remove her dress. You might want to go home and get her something to wear while I'm treating her."

Cameron couldn't leave if he wanted to. His heart was in his throat and his jaw set so he wouldn't scream. "I'm not leaving. I'll take her home in the blanket you cover her with."

"All right. Let me get to work."

Together, they removed Eve's dress, her corset, her camisole and Cameron put her derringer in his pocket. His hands shook as he saw the blood oozing from her body.

Doc checked the exit wound on the left side of her right breast. "It looks like her corset saved her. The bullet hit the boning, and the trajectory was to the right, missing her heart and her lungs. If she had to be shot, this was the best possible outcome."

"So, the baby is safe?" asked Cameron.

"Yes, the baby is safe as long as Eve doesn't get an infection from the bullet, *both* of them should be just fine."

"Eve wants this baby so badly and I do, too, but I want Eve safe more than anything. We can have other children."

Doc nodded. "I'm glad to hear it. I was worried when you didn't ask if Eve was safe before you asked about the baby."

He felt guilty that he didn't ask about Eve to begin with. "I just assumed Eve would recover if the baby was all right. I guess it did sound a little callous. But I know that is the first thing she'll ask is if the baby is all right."

"Yes, it did sound callous. Now, I'll pour alcohol in her wounds to kill any thing left by the bullet. It should stop any infections, but they're still possible. She's unconscious right now, but the pain from the alcohol might wake her. I want you to hold her down."

Cameron walked around the table to the head and pressed her shoulders so she couldn't move.

Doc poured the liquid into the wound.

Eve woke and screamed, then cried.

Cameron's heart broke. He would do anything to take the pain for her. "It's okay, Eve. Sweetheart, you'll be fine. The baby is fine. Can you hear me, Eve? I love you. You'll be fine. Do you hear me?"

"She's passed out again Cameron and that's a good thing. Sewing up the wound is painful. Not as much as the alcohol, but still painful." Doc Whitaker sewed up the wound quickly. "I've used as small a stitch as I could so the scarring shouldn't be too bad. Help me turn her over. You'll have to hold her down again."

He nodded, prepared for her to scream again, but instead she just cried harder.

"Eve, sweetheart, the baby is fine. A couple of little scars is all you'll have to remember this day."

"Okay." She managed to say over her sniffles.

"Are you ready to go home, sweetheart?"

She nodded and turned her head away.

The doctor tore off the end of a bandage and dabbed at the wound. "Okay, I've gotten her all sewed up. I'll give her a dose of laudanum here and I want you to give her another one at home and again in three to four hours, but don't wake her to give it to her. Sleep is the best thing for her now. Use more of the laudanum I gave you. The instructions are the same as with her ankle." Doc wrapped her shoulder with clean bandages.

"I'll let her sleep as much as possible."

Doc nodded. "For at least three or four days she should take it. Every three hours for the first two days and then you can slowly wean her off it over the next three days."

"Okay."

The doctor mixed the laudanum and gave it to her. "That's right drink it down. All of it. Good girl." He removed the glass. "You can take her home now. Put her directly to bed and I want her to stay there for at least four days. Understand?"

"Yes. That's the second time you've told me. I've got it. Brandi will watch her during the day and I'll watch her at night. She won't be left alone."

"Good."

"I'll bring your blanket back."

"I'm not worried about it. I have more."

Cameron nodded, covered Eve with the blanket and lifted her into his arms.

Doc held the door for him.

He stopped before leaving the building. "Put this visit on my bill. I'll pay you in full at the end of the month."

"Of course," said Doc. "I expect to hear immediately if she develops a fever or if you see any yellow discharge from the wound. That will indicate infection, and I'll have to open it and clean it out."

"Will do, Doc. Now, I just want to get her home."

"Yes. I'll come by tomorrow to see how she's doing and to bring you more bandages. I want them changed every other day."

"Thanks again, Doc."

Cameron walked home with an unconscious Eve

in his arms. "You'll be fine. You must. I love you, and I can't lose you. And we have a baby coming. You'll be fine." He looked skyward. "Please, God, let her be all right."

He got her home and walked to the front door.

Brandi opened the door as he approached. "I've been watching for you. Robert Lee came by and your deputies arrested all three Stone brothers. They're in jail now and can't cause any more harm."

She ran ahead of him and turned down the covers.

He unwrapped Eve from the blanket and laid her in the bed, covering her and tucking her in. Then he pulled a chair to the bedside, grabbed his book from the nightstand and waited for Eve to awaken.

Brandi came into the room carrying two cups. "I brought you some coffee." She set her cup on the bureau and went to her room and got the chair bringing it back to the bedside, opposite of Cameron.

"You don't have to stay." Cameron said.

Brandi cocked her head and narrowed her eyes. "Don't tell me what I have to do or don't have to do. She means as much to me, probably more, than she means to you. I love her. She's the sister I never had. She saved me." The girl reached over and took Eve's hand in hers.

Cameron noticed the tears running down Brandi's face. "I didn't mean to keep you from her. I just thought," he sighed. "Ah, heck, I don't know what I meant. Doc says she'll be okay. The bullet went clear through so he didn't have to dig it out, thank God, but that doesn't mean I'm not still scared." He told her what the doctor said about watching the wound.

"I can help you change her bandages and look for infection."

Cameron took a deep breath and was about to tell her no, but then he saw her face and knew she needed to care for Eve as much as he did. "I'd appreciate the help. Two sets of eyes are always better than one."

She nodded and smiled. "I've always thought so."

He reached into his pocket and pulled out Eve's derringer. "Here you might need this, too."

Brandi walked around the bed and put the gun in her left pocket. She had the Colt in her right.

"You never know when you might need both guns and don't be afraid to use them." He looked down at his wife. *Please Eve. Wake up and talk to me. Tell me you hate me, anything, just wake up.*

CHAPTER SIXTEEN

*E*ve woke slowly, grimacing with pain.

"Eve. Sweetheart. How are you feeling?"

She kept her eyes closed. "Like I've been shot… from a cannon."

Cameron chuckled.

Brandi laughed.

"I'd say you'll be all right. Your sense of humor is intact," said Cameron. "Will you open your eyes?"

"Nope."

"Why not?" asked Brandi.

"Because then all this will be real. Now it's just a dream…a bad dream, but a dream nonetheless." Cameron squeezed her hand lightly.

"Sweetheart, open your eyes. I need to know you can see."

She shook her head. "I was shot in the back. What does that have to do with my eyes?"

"I don't know. Just humor me," he said.

He sounded exasperated, so she slowly opened her eyes. The room was dark except for the lamps on the nightstands. "How long have I been out?"

"Almost eight hours. We were wondering if we'd have to wake you."

"I guess I needed the rest." She placed her hands on her stomach. Her eyes widened and her brows furrowed. "The baby?"

Cameron covered her hands with one of his. "The baby is fine. Doc said the bullet didn't come anywhere near the baby."

She let out a deep breath. "Thank God."

"Are you hungry?" asked Brandi.

Eve looked over at her. "Have you been here the whole time, too?"

Brandi nodded. "Well, except for the time I was making chicken soup. It should be ready now if you'd like some. Maybe just a cup instead of a bowl, until we're sure you can keep it down."

"Yes." Eve smiled at her friend. "I think a cup is a good idea. And maybe with some soda crackers."

Brandi stood. "Coming right up." She hurried out of the room.

Eve turned to Cameron. Her wound throbbed

worse when she tried to move so she stayed as still as possible.

He looked at her with a smile.

"Why are you looking at me like that?"

"Like what?"

"Like the cat who got the cream."

"I'm just happy you're alive, that's all."

She turned away. "You mean because of the baby."

"Eve, look at me."

She shook her head, not wanting to hear his confirmation that he only cared about the baby.

"Please, sweetheart."

What was the matter with her hearing? Did she want to hear loving words from him so much that she was making every word he said sound loving?

She looked at him. "Why are you calling me that?"

He lifted his brows. "What?"

"You know. Why are you calling me sweetheart?"

He chuckled. "Because you are my sweetheart. I discovered something about myself when you were shot."

"Oh, what was that?"

He stood and sat on the bed next to her. "I discovered that I'm a hypocrite. I wasn't willing to do something I expected you to do."

She lowered her chin and narrowed her eyes. "What was that?"

His gaze never left hers. "I realized that I love you, but I was waiting for you to tell me first. That's hypocritical. I love you, Eve, and if you don't love me yet, I believe with all my heart you will because this feeling I have inside is too strong to be one-sided. And I have enough love for the both of us until you decide you love me, too."

Eve's heart pounded and her pulse raced. She grinned and reached for his hand. "I do love you. I've been waiting for you to realize you love me before I told you, so I guess I'm a hypocrite, too."

"We've wasted so much time. I won't waste another minute." He leaned over and kissed her, loving her with his lips.

She groaned. A sharp pain radiated through her as she tried to put her arms around him.

He pulled back. "What's wrong? Did I hurt you?"

Eve shook her head. "You didn't hurt me. This dang wound hurt me. I think I need more laudanum, please."

"I know and I'm sorry. Why don't you try to rest? Brandi will be here with soup for you in a bit and you'll feel better. You've been asleep long enough that I can give you another dose without worry. It's dangerous stuff and I don't want to hurt the baby. Try and relax." He mixed the medicine for her and watched her drink it. Then he rubbed her arm up and down.

The slow motion felt wonderful. Eve closed her eyes. "I may have to eat it later."

Cameron held her hand until she was asleep, then he went to the kitchen. "Brandi, will you watch Eve in case she wakes up while I'm gone? I have to file the paperwork for the Stone brothers, and I want to make sure they're in jail, locked up good and tight."

Brandi jumped a little when he entered. When he mentioned the Stone brothers, she furrowed her brows and pursed her lips. "Do you think they might escape?"

"I don't know. One of the things Buck Stone is wanted for is escaping prison. I'll feel better if I confirm for myself he's safe behind bars."

"I'm keeping Eve's derringer. If he comes here, I'll shoot him. No questions asked and just as soon as he gets close enough."

"Agreed."

"I should hold it to George and get him to marry me. But I hope I don't have to use it against Buck Stone or any of the brothers. I'm not a killer but I won't let them in to be beat up again and probably killed this time."

Cameron clinched his jaw. "I hope you don't have to use it either. I'll be back in about a half hour. Don't let anyone in besides me."

"Or George. He's supposed to come by in about ten minutes."

"Be very careful and make sure it's George before you open that door."

"I will, even though the Stone brothers are in jail."

"You definitely do that. Buck Stone is dangerous. His brothers are sheep and follow his lead. But Buck, I need to put an extra guard on just for him."

"We'll be fine. Just hurry back."

"As fast as I can."

Cameron left out the kitchen door.

———

*B*randi locked it after him and then ran to the front door and made sure it was still locked. After that she checked the soup in the kitchen. She put it on the back burner to simmer, then went to check on Eve.

———

*E*ve was awake and trying to get out of bed. Brandi hurried to her side. "Here, let me help you."

"Thanks, I feel so weak. Just sitting up took major effort. If I didn't need to relieve myself, I wouldn't be getting up at all." She leaned on Brandi.

She put her arm around Eve's waist. "I understand. I felt the same way after Buck and his brothers got done with me. But I had to tell Rose what happened and that I couldn't work for a while."

When she was finished, Brandi helped Eve back into bed.

"How are you feeling, pain wise?"

"My pain feels like it's coming back. I think the laudanum is wearing off."

"Do you want me to get you some more?"

"No. I really don't want to get hooked on the stuff."

"How about I read to you?"

"No, thanks." She shook her head. "I don't know what I want. I feel sad for no reason."

Brandi took Eve's hand. "It's not for no reason. You were shot. I want you to keep this gun with you." She handed her the Colt that Cameron had given her. "You just never know when you might need it."

Eve nodded and took the revolver Brandi handed her. "Yeah, I suppose that's true." She took the gun and placed it under the covers next to her.

A knock sounded on the front door.

Brandi looked at Eve. "I've got your derringer. Cameron gave it to me after he brought you back. You keep that Colt, it's too heavy for me anyway, so you keep it…just in case." She hurried from the room.

*S*topping in the living room, Brandi put her ear to the front door. "Who's there?"

"It's George."

Brandi smiled and unlocked the door.

George came flying into the room.

The next thing she knew, Buck Stone was standing in front of her. "Where is she? Where's that witch who stole my money?"

Shocked that Buck Stone was standing there, she worried about Cameron and Robert. Where were they? "She's not here. You shot her, remember."

"She's here. The doctor was more forthcoming when I threatened to shoot his patient, a pregnant woman who looked like she was about to give birth."

"You're an evil man, Buck Stone." Brandi didn't back away. She reached into her pocket.

"Don't sass me. This is what you like." He backhanded her, sending her crashing to the floor.

"Stop that! Don't you hit her." George charged Buck.

Buck sidestepped him and hit the butt of his gun on the back of George's head as he passed by.

George fell to the floor, unconscious.

Brandi stood with the derringer aimed at Buck. "You've been warned." She fired the little gun.

The bullet hit Buck in the right side of his belly.

He looked down and touched the wound with his left hand. It came away bloody. "Why, you—" He lifted his gun and aimed it at Brandi.

A shot rang out.

Brandi expected to feel more pain…heck, any pain.

Buck Stone fell to the floor, a bullet in his brain.

Brandi swung around and looked behind her.

Eve stood with Cameron's Colt in her hand, smoke coming from the end of the barrel. She swayed and leaned against the wall.

"Eve!" Brandi ran to catch her before she slid down to the floor. As it turned out, both ended up on the floor.

*H*earing a gunshot, panic filled Cameron as he ran into the house through the open door and saw his wife. "Eve, sweetheart." He knelt in front of her and Brandi.

"I'm fine," said Eve. She grinned at Brandi. "We're fine."

Brandi stood. "I'll check on George. If he's not hurt too bad I'll help him to the kitchen."

Relief coursing through him, Cameron nodded and then picked Eve up in his arms and stood. He carried her to their bedroom and laid her back in the middle of the bed. "Are you sure you're fine? The baby?"

"Is fine. We're both happy Buck Stone is dead. How did he escape?"

Cameron sat on the edge of the bed, facing her, his right hand on her leg. "When I got to the jail, he was already gone, his brothers are dead. Robert Lee was lying unconscious in the office with a gunshot wound. Apparently, Sam Chism helped Buck escape. I don't know what Buck promised him and never will since he's dead in the jail with the Stone brothers. It looks like Sam gave Buck a gun and let him out. Then Buck shot Sam. Buck fired on Robert as he went into the back to see what was happening with the gun shots.

Robert fired at Buck and hit at least one of the brothers. Then Sam, after being shot by Buck, killed the other brother, before dying himself.

"And Robert?" asked Eve as she slumped down even lower into the mattress. "Will he recover?"

"I don't know. That will be for Doc to determine, but I think so. He was conscious and talking when I left. Doc had already been notified of the gunfire and was headed into the jail as I was headed out."

Eve shook her head slowly. "I hope so, for his family's sake. He has a brand-new son. That baby can't be losing his daddy so soon."

"I know."

"I'm tired now."

"Do you want me to get you some laudanum?"

"No, what I want is for you to come here and hold me. I need to feel your arms around me. I've never killed anyone before."

He stood and gave her a kiss. "I know but before I do that, and believe me, I want to hold you more than anything, but now that I know you're all right, I have to get that vermin out of our living room and tell the undertaker we have a body to be picked up…from our porch. I'm not having that scum in our house any longer than I have to."

"I understand. I'll be waiting for you when you get back."

"I won't be gone long, my love."

"Just do what you have to do. The sooner I'm in your arms the better."

"My thoughts, exactly."

Cameron picked Buck up under his arms and dragged him, with his head lolling on his chest so blood didn't get everywhere, out the door. He dropped him on the side of the porch.

Then he went to the kitchen.

Brandi was there, doctoring George.

"How are you, George?" Cameron laid a hand on his shoulder. "He didn't hurt you too bad, did he?"

He shook his head. "Not bad at all."

"Not true." Brandi put her hands on her hips. "You have a knot on your head the size of a goose egg, and one of your eyes is bloodshot. I want the doctor to look at him, and he's refusing."

"You should have the doc check you out. I'd hate to see you two get married, and you keel over the next day."

Brandi grinned at Cameron over the top of George's head.

"Fine, I'll have Doc look at it and then we can get married. If this day has shown me anything, it's that life is short." He looked up at Brandi, who stood beside him with a washcloth in her hand. "We're getting married, tomorrow, if we can. I won't be takin' no for an answer, Brandi Johnson."

She grinned from ear to ear. "Yes, George. What-ever you say."

"I hope you'll consider waiting until Eve is mobile. She would hate to miss your wedding. I think Judge Ralston will do it any time you want." Cameron lifted a brow. "Maybe you can even do it here. The judge owes me."

Brandi burst into laughter. "That he does."

George cocked his head. "What's so funny?"

She dropped the washcloth into the basin on the

table. "Nothing, darling. I'll tell you during our drive. Do you have the buggy outside?"

"I do. Shall we go?"

"Yes, let's. We can talk about when we'll get married."

He took her hand and tucked it into the crook of his arm. "I can't wait."

Cameron smiled at the young lovers then he went to get the undertaker.

Now that he and Eve knew they loved each other, he couldn't wait to make love to her. Real love. Too bad they had to wait for ten days.

*E*ve couldn't wait to get her stitches out. She'd had them in for ten days now. She and Cameron sat in Doc's waiting room.

"Eve, you can come back now."

She and Cameron stood and went back to the examination room.

Doc shook his head. "Do I have both of you to look forward to at each visit during your pregnancy?"

"No, Doc, don't worry," said Cameron. "I'll be out of your hair as soon as I make sure Eve is recovered."

Eve sat on the exam table.

"Based on my observation of your wife kicking

her feet like a little girl, I'd say she is probably recovered just fine." He turned toward Eve. "What do you say? Shall I take your stitches out?"

"Oh, yes, Doc. Please take them out." Eve was already unbuttoning her blouse.

"All right. Just hold your horses." Doc walked over to one side of the room and the short counter with cupboards and drawers that was mounted to the wall there. He washed his hands and brought a damp towel over to the table where Eve sat. "Hold this."

Doc went to work on her back first, snipping those ten stitches.

She felt every stitch since they tickled when they came out. Not so some of the sixteen in front. The exit wound was bigger and the skin had grown around some of the stitches and he had to cut the skin away before he removed the stitch. The wound bled and doc put a bandage back on. "Keep this on until the bleeding stops, then you can take it off and let the injuries heal uncovered unless they start bleeding again. I suggest that if you can, wear dark clothing until you're sure they won't bleed."

Eve buttoned her blouse and hopped off the table. "Thank you, Doc. I'll have Cameron check me every morning and night to make sure the wound is healing properly, and I'll be back here if it's not."

Cameron came forward, hand outstretched. "Thanks, Doc. What do I owe you?"

"Treatment of a bullet wound is five dollars."

Cameron paid him and then took Eve's hand. "Bye, Doc."

"Yes," said Eve. "Bye, and I hope I don't see you again until my first pregnancy checkup."

"That sounds very good." Doc smiled. "Now, get on out of here." He shooed them out with his hands.

As they walked home, Eve leaned into Cameron. "We can really start our marriage now. All our cards are on the table, so to speak."

Cameron grimaced. "No more gambling references. I don't want you to ever gamble for a living again. And if I do something that makes you that angry, talk to me about it before you don that red dress again. Although, I admit, that dress is the sexiest one I've ever seen."

"It's ruined anyway with the bullet hole in it." She sighed, just a little sad to let the dress go. The garment had been with her for too many years. "I had it made special. I told the seamstress what I wanted. She said she wouldn't have a problem designing a dress I would love...and she was right. The garment was perfect. It showed plenty without showing too much." She laughed. "It gave me a distinct advantage at the poker table."

"I bet it did." He stopped walking at the end of the path to their house. "I love you, Eve. I'll make sure you never have to live in that dangerous way again. Our children will have a normal mama."

Eve reached up and brought his head down to her. She kissed him with all the love she felt deep in her heart. "I want you to build a fire when we get home."

"All right, whatever you want."

When they arrived home, Cameron built a nice fire in the living room.

A few minutes later, Eve came out of their bedroom carrying the red dress.

"This is the last time you'll ever see this dress." She tossed the dress into the fireplace. Then she took Cameron's hand, sat on the sofa and together they watched it burn.

In some ways she was sad to say goodbye to something, to a way of life that connected her to her father. But now she had so much more. She had Cameron and a baby on the way. She had a best friend in Brandi, someone she'd never had before.

Eve may not have the connection to her father but she had so much more and she knew she'd never be alone again.

*J*anuary 29, 1864

The Neal home, 9:00 o'clock in the evening

*E*ve was changing into her night clothes when she felt the warm liquid run down the inside of her legs. Excitement filled her. The wait was finally over, her babe was on the way. "Cameron! Cameron!"

"I'm here." He rushed into the bedroom.

"My water just broke. The baby is coming." Her first real pain gripped her, but she didn't want to let Cameron know. She'd had a backache all last night and today, but didn't associate it with labor until now.

"I'll go get Doc."

She got a towel from the commode and wiped her legs. "Not yet. According to Methabel Lee, the wait for the baby is just beginning and could be hours yet before the little one decides to show his face. I'll let you know when. I think you can get Brandi. She and George can come over now, if they want, and stop at the Ralstons and notify them. I'll need Blanche."

Cameron walked over to her. "Will you be all right until we return?"

"I'll be fine." She reached out and cupped his face. "Actually, I think I'll bake some cookies. It will keep me busy and keep my mind off the pain."

He kissed her.

He made love to her with his mouth. She pulled back. "Go on, now. I'll be here when you return."

"All right, I'm leaving. We'll be back in a little while."

"See you then."

After he left, she let herself grimace with the pain. Then she slipped her dress on over her nightgown and prepared the bed for the birth by removing the sheets and blankets, putting down the oilcloth and covering it with a sheet. Then she went to the kitchen. By the time Cameron returned with the Clarendons, she was putting two pans of sugar cookies in the oven.

"Shouldn't you be in bed?" Brandi grabbed a pinch of cookie dough and popped it in her mouth.

Cameron got cups for the four of them and set them on the table. Then he picked up a hot pad and retrieved the coffee pot from the stove. He filled the cups, put the pot back, and sat. "Eve, come sit after you get that pan in the oven."

"I will. Just a minute." She checked the pans of cookies in the oven and then sat on Cameron's right side.

Her husband raised his coffee cup. "I'd like to propose a toast."

Everyone raised their cup.

Cameron turned toward her and smiled. "To my lovely bride. I never expected to find someone I would love so much or to be as happy as I am. Thank you, Eve, for answering the ad Earl placed in the paper."

Her eyes filled with tears at his sweet words. She swiped at her cheeks. "I've never been so happy to have read the paper, but I can't really take credit for it. Daniel saw the ad and gave me the paper so I could get out of town and lie low. That's all this marriage was supposed to be, but it turned into so much more than I ever could have imagined. I love you." Suddenly, she set her cup down on the table and squeezed her eyes shut. She moaned and rocked back and forth on the chair.

"Eve? Is there something I can do to help?" asked Cameron.

Eve shook her head as the pain subsided. She relaxed against the back of the chair and breathed in a shaky breath. "I love you for asking but you can't help me with this. It was just a contraction. Doc said these first ones won't last long and will come far apart. When they get closer together, like every five minutes or so, then someone should go get him."

"Okay. Let's begin timing them." He looked at his pocket watch. "That one happened at eight-fifteen."

Eve nodded and clasped her hands on the tabletop. "Good. Now, George, tell us how the new session is going at school?"

He smiled and reached for Brandi's hand where it lay on the table. "Very well. The students are so happy to learn. They are just like sponges and absorb everything I can teach them. Pretty soon, they'll know more than I do."

"How can that be if they are learning only what you teach them?" Cameron asked.

"Well," responded George. "They all have knowledge of farming, ranching, or mining, through their parents and in some cases through their own experiences." He went on to explain a couple of recent lessons.

"It's wonderful you have such a rewarding job," said Eve. "Cameron is the same way. Keeping this town safe for people like you and me is difficult. I didn't know how hard that job was when we first got married. Oh!" She closed her eyes for a bit and breathed through her mouth. "I think I need to lie down."

"Well," said Cameron, "That was only ten minutes since the last one. Should you be having contractions so close together to begin with?"

Eve reached up her hand and cupped his jaw. "I've been having them most of the evening. I didn't say anything because you can't do anything to help, but now I think you should go get Doc."

Cameron jumped to his feet. His eyes wide. "Whatever you say. I'll be right back."

He left out the back door.

"Brandi, would you come back to the bedroom with me?"

"Of course." She stood and turned to her husband. "Wait in the living room for me, please, and I'll be back in a bit."

George stood. He towered over Brandi, but the difference didn't seem to matter. He bent and kissed her. "I'll be there, trying to read, but more than likely I'll be pacing."

Brandi laughed. "If you're this anxious now, you'll be a total wreck when our baby comes." She touched her rounded belly.

George visibly paled. "I don't even want to think about it."

Eve laughed. "Your time is coming soon enough,

just a few months now. Come on, let's go. I need to lie down." She left the kitchen and headed to her bedroom. Eve didn't make it to the bedroom before another pain hit her. She stopped, braced a hand on the wall and the other on her belly. She tried to breathe through the pain but it was exceedingly difficult.

Brandi was quickly beside her. "Here we go. Lean on me."

Eve laughed. "I can't lean on you, you're too short."

Brandi laughed, too. "Fine. I'll hold you by the waist." She wrapped an arm around Eve's back.

They walked into the bedroom.

Eve immediately removed her dress and revealed her nightgown.

"You definitely are ready for this little one."

"I am *so* ready. I'm so tired of being pregnant." Eve arranged the pillows for her back and laid on the bed. "Ah. Right now, lying down feels wonderful. You can't imagine how good being on this bed feels, at least until another one hits. But you will. In just a few months, you'll be where I am." She stopped for a moment and looked at her dearest friend. "Are you okay, Brandi?"

She lifted her strawberry blonde head. Her eyes were closed and her brows almost came together. "What? I'm fine. Why would you think otherwise?"

"I don't know. Maybe because you're grimacing. You're having your first baby, too, and that can be a difficult time for women. I hope you know you can talk to me whenever you want."

Brandi cocked her head and smiled. "I'll remind you of that when you are in the throes of delivering your baby."

Eve laughed. "You will, too. Forgive me if I don't respond with anything but a grunt, moan or scream."

She grinned. "I'll forgive you anything."

Eve's eyes misted. *He should be here to hold my hand.* "Where the heck is Cameron with that doctor?"

"I'm here." He rushed to her side. "Doc Whitaker is right behind me."

The doctor, tufts of white hair sticking out from under his hat, entered the room. "I'm here. I'm a little slower than I used to be, but not enough that this young pup," he pointed at Cameron, "can leave me that far behind. Now, tell me what's happening to you this minute."

"Nothing, but I just finished having a bad contraction. I've been in labor for about twenty-four hours, but my water didn't break until just two hours ago. Now my contractions are coming about every five minutes…" She closed her eyes and blew out puffs of air through her mouth, as another contraction hit. "Or less. I think I'm ready to have this baby, Doc."

"All right." He looked at Cameron. "It's time for you to go to the living room with George."

"I don't want to leave her." Cameron gazed at Eve. "I want to help you in any way I can."

She lifted a hand and caressed his cheek. "Go, I'll be fine. Brandi is here and Blanche is coming. Earl will want you with him. Really. Go."

He leaned down and kissed her soundly. "I'm only leaving because you insist."

"Yes, I do."

Cameron straightened his spine and walked out of the room, but he stopped at the door and turned back toward her.

She smiled and cocked her head. "Go."

When he was gone, she moaned with pain. "Doc, why does it hurt so much? Why would anyone do this to themselves again…for any reason?"

Doc chuckled. "When you have your baby in your arms, you won't remember any of the pain. Trust me."

Blanche came into the room. "Where do you want me, Doc?"

"Brandi, I want you to hold the lamp. Blanche, you get ready to wash the baby."

"All right now, let's have a look and see when that baby is coming."

The room got quiet and then the doctor exclaimed. "Jumpin' Jehoshaphat! Your baby is coming on it's own. Eve, push, *NOW*. Push! That's right keep it up. Push."

She reached behind her and grabbed the headboard for purchase and pushed for all she was worth and wished she'd had Cameron stay. This circumstance was all his fault, and he should darn well be there to go through it with her.

"Push! Just once more. Hard, Eve, hard as you can."

She pushed and soon felt the baby's body slide from hers. She blew out a sigh of relief. "What is it? What do I have?"

The doctor cleaned the baby's mouth out with his finger and then, when the baby didn't make a noise, he swatted it on the bottom.

The little one hollered.

Eve had never heard a sweeter sound in her whole life. "Doc?"

"Blanche, take her please. I must deliver the afterbirth."

Blanche grinned. Before she walked to the bureau, she said, "You have a beautiful little daughter. She appears to have dark hair, like her daddy, and we'll wait to see what color eyes she has. Most likely they'll be blue now, but the color could change as she grows older."

Brandi held the lamp for the doctor as he delivered the afterbirth and put it into a bucket just for that purpose.

Cameron appeared at the door. His hair was wild, like he'd been running his hands back and forth through it. "I heard a baby cry. Eve, are you okay?"

She smiled, more tired and more exhilarated than she'd ever been in her whole life. "I'm fine, my love. We have a daughter."

"A girl? A baby…girl?" He sat on the bed next to her side.

"Yes, a girl." Her heart felt lodged in her throat "Are you disappointed?" Eve asked.

"What? Disappointed? No." Cameron laughed. "I'm thrilled. I wanted a little girl who looks like her mama. Does she?"

Eve laughed. His laughter was a balm to her soul. "Actually, she looks like her daddy."

Cameron sighed and then laughed. "Oh, the poor thing."

Eve tried to swat him, but her energy was spent.

Blanche brought the baby over. "There you go, Mama."

"Thank you." She lifted her arms and accepted her daughter who weighed so little. "For everything." Never taking her eyes from her daughter, she unwrapped the baby she loved since she knew of her existence.

She and Cameron counted fingers and toes.

"What do you want to call her?" he asked. Then he leaned down and kissed Eve almost reverently.

"I thought we would call her Elinore...Ellie. Elinore Blanche Neal."

Cameron grinned as Ellie wrapped her little fingers around the tip of his finger. "I like it."

Blanche stopped cleaning up the bureau and turned toward them. "Did you say, Blanche? After me?"

"Yup, you were more like a mother to me than the mother I had," said Cameron.

Tears rolled, unfettered, down Blanche's cheeks. "I can't believe it. I'm so honored...so happy. Earl will never believe it. I must go tell him." She ran to the bed and kissed Cameron, Eve and Ellie. Then she ran out of the room.

Ellie began to fuss. Her arms and legs jerking around.

Eve smiled at her child. "I think she's cold."

"Can I see her?" asked Brandi, quietly.

"Of course." Eve wrapped Ellie back up. "You'll have one just like her, well maybe a boy, but still a baby—"

"You're rambling, sweetheart." Cameron kissed her.

Brandi looked down at Ellie and her mouth ticked up. "She's so beautiful." Then she laughed. "Yes, I will have a baby in a few months. I can't wait, even seeing the pain you went through, I'm still excited. She is so worth it."

"You should go get George," said Eve.

Brandi handed Ellie to Cameron. "We'll come back later. I think you three should have some time together."

Eve lifted a hand toward Brandi.

The woman came over and clasped Eve's hand in both of hers.

"Thank you, sister of my heart," said Eve. "I will always be grateful that I sat at the same table as Daniel Calhoun, otherwise I would never have met you."

"You scared me, I thought you were going to say the Stone brothers."

"In a way, them, too. If they hadn't bragged of how bad they had been to you, I wouldn't have found you either. So, yes, I'm grateful I sat at the same table they did. I'll never be grateful for what they did to you. As a matter of fact, I've never been happier that someone was dead. But you came with me when you didn't have to. You could have stayed, found a job as a maid or something."

Brandi shook her head and then laughed. "I don't ever want to work that hard. I'll see you tomorrow, and I'll tell Blanche, too, that Earl can see you tomorrow."

"I think that's a wonderful idea," said Doc

Whitaker. He picked up his bag and the bucket. "I'll see you tomorrow myself."

Cameron stood and offered his hand. "Thanks, Doc. What do I owe you?"

Doc shook his hand. "You already paid the fee with her checkups."

Cameron pulled a five-dollar gold piece from his pocket. "Take this as a tip or as a down payment on the next one."

"Next one! Now, hold on, buster," said Eve, her eyes narrowed. "I just had Ellie. I'm not ready to discuss another one anytime soon."

He leaned over, kissed her and then sat next to her on the bed. "Just teasing, my love, just teasing."

Doc chuckled. "See you both tomorrow."

"Bye, Doc." Eve and Cameron said it together.

When the door was closed and they were finally alone, Eve stared at her little Ellie. As warmth spread through her chest, hot tears filled her eyes. "She's so beautiful. I never knew I could love someone so much."

"I know," said Cameron. "I didn't either. Thank you, Eve."

The tears rolled down her cheeks. "For what?"

He looked down at her, his lips trembling. "For taking a chance on me. For giving us a chance and for our beautiful daughter. I don't know how I'll ever thank you."

The terrible trip to get to Silver City, the danger from the Stone brothers, all paled in her memory as she looked up at her husband and then down at her precious daughter. "I'm sure I'll think of a way. I love you, Cameron."

"I love you more, Eve."

Newsletter

Sign up for my newsletter and get a free book.

Follow Cindy

https://www.facebook.com/cindy.woolf.5
https://twitter.com/CynthiaWoolf
http://cynthiawoolf.com

ABOUT THE AUTHOR

Cynthia Woolf is an award-winning and best-selling author of fifty-one historical western romance novels and six sci-fi romance novels, which she calls westerns in space. Along with these books she has also published four boxed sets of her books.

Cynthia loves writing and reading romance. Her first western romance Tame A Wild Heart was inspired by the story her mother told her of meeting Cynthia's father on a ranch in Creede, Colorado. Although Tame A Wild Heart takes place in Creede that is the only similarity between the stories. Her father was a cowboy not a bounty hunter and her mother was a nursemaid (called a nanny now) not the owner of the ranch.

Cynthia credits her wonderfully supportive husband Jim and her great critique partners for saving her sanity and allowing her to explore her creativity.

Bachelors and Babies

Carter

Cupids & Cowboys

Lanie

The Marshal's Mail Order Brides

The Carson City Bride

The Virginia City Bride

The Silver City Bride

Brides of Homestead Canyon/Montana Sky Series

Thorpe's Mail-Order Bride

Kissed by a Stranger

A Family for Christmas

Bride of Nevada

Genevieve

Brides of the Oregon Trail

Hannah

Lydia

Bella

Eliza

Rebecca

Charlotte

Brides of San Francisco

Nellie

Annie

Cora

Sophia

Amelia

Brides of Seattle

Mail Order Mystery

Mail Order Mayhem

Mail Order Mix-Up

Mail Order Moonlight

Mail Order Melody

Brides of Tombstone

Mail Order Outlaw

Mail Order Doctor

Mail Order Baron

Central City Brides

The Dancing Bride

The Sapphire Bride

The Irish Bride

The Pretender Bride

Destiny in Deadwood

Jake

Liam

Zach

Hope's Crossing

The Stolen Bride

The Hunter Bride

The Replacement Bride

The Unexpected Bride

Matchmaker & Co Series

Capital Bride

Heiress Bride

Fiery Bride

Colorado Bride

The Surprise Brides

Gideon

Tame

Tame a Wild Heart

Tame a Wild Wind

Tame a Wild Bride

Tame A Honeymoon Heart

Tame Boxset

Centauri Series (SciFi Romance)

Centauri Dawn

Centauri Twilight

Centauri Midnight

Singles

Sweetwater Springs Christmas

Made in the USA
Coppell, TX
21 April 2022